THE UNIQUE MAGAZINE
SPRING 1991

ISSN 0898-5073
Art by Gahan Wilson

*Weird Tales®* is published 4 times a year by Terminus Publishing Co., Inc., PO Box 13418, Philadelphia PA 19101-3418 (4426 Larchwood Ave., Philadelphia PA 19014-3916). 2nd Class Postage paid at Philadelphia PA & additional mailing offices. Single copies, $4.95. Subscriptions: 4 issues (one year) $16.00 in U.S.A. & possessions; $20.00 in Canada & Mexico, $22.00 elsewhere, in U.S. funds. Publisher is not responsible for loss of manuscripts, although publisher will take reasonable care of them. Postmaster: send address changes to *Weird Tales®*, PO Box 13418, Philadelphia PA 19101-3418. Copyright © 1991 by Terminus Publishing Co., Inc.; all rights reserved; reproduction prohibited without prior permission. Typeset, printed, & bound in the United States of America. Weird Tales® is a registered trademark owned by Weird Tales, Limited.

# THE EYRIE

**Welcome to the 300th issue of Weird Tales®!** This time we are particularly pleased to honor one of the magazine's most distinguished contributors, *Robert Bloch*, whose first professional sales, "The Feast in the Abbey" and "The Secret of the Tomb" appeared here in 1935. He sold over a hundred stories in the following decade, many of them to *Weird Tales®*, including the classic "Yours Truly, Jack the Ripper." He was honored as the only writer to meet a hideous doom at the hands (or tentacles, or Three-Lobed Burning Eye) of Nyarlathotep in a story by H.P. Lovecraft (as "Robert Blake" in "The Haunter of the Dark," December 1936). His earliest horror stories are in a Lovecraftian mode. He soon became fascinated by the lore of ancient Egypt, as evidenced by "Beetles" in this issue. He rapidly loosened up a bit, wrote less traditional stories in a more modern style with lots of deft dialogue, branched out to humor, perpetrated the famous (or infamous) Lefty Feep series for *Fantastic Adventures* (and some humorous stories for *Weird Tales®*); moved on to radio; became the Thomas Harris of the '40s, '50s, and '60s with such novels as *The Scarf, The Dead Beat,* and *Firebug*; wrote science fiction including the classic "The Strange Flight of Richard Clayton" and several novels; turned to film and TV; wrote hundreds more stories collected in dozens of books from the 1945 Arkham House *The Opener of the Way* to the recent, gargantuan matched set of *The Selected Stories of Robert Bloch*; returned to novels with *Lori, The Ripper Legacy*, and others for Tor Books; and has unquestionably become, after fifty-plus years of writing, scads of awards, and the much-deserved adulation of his peers which took the form of a Life Achievement Award from the Horror Writers of America last summer, one of the most distinguished living practitioners of what we variously call Dark Fantasy, Suspense, or just plain scary stuff. There are precious few people more deserving of a special issue of *Weird Tales®* than Robert Bloch.

Quite incidentally, he's also the author of *Psycho*; but you probably knew that already.

And this just in: we will soon be publishing two *new* Robert Bloch stories, which were received too late for inclusion in this issue.

**The Last of Henry Kuttner:** The story "The Grab Bag" in this issue also represents what we suspect will be the *final* first appearance of another *Weird*

I0535841

*Tales*® discovery, *Henry Kuttner*, whose first story, "The Graveyard Rats", appeared here in March 1936. Kuttner had an extremely distinguished career, more in science fiction than in horror, and died in 1958. He collaborated with Robert Bloch several times in the early '40s, when "The Grab Bag" was written. This story, however, has never been published anywhere until now.

**Staff Changes:** Astute readers of the magazine's masthead will note several changes this time, the most dramatic of which is the departure of John Betancourt from the editors/publishers merry-go-round. (We always rotated the names to emphasize the equality of the three partners. There was no senior editor.) With the press of his novel-writing career and his full-time job as an editor at Byron Preiss Visual Productions, not to mention his removal to Newark while the magazine is published in Philadelphia, John has simply been unable to continue with *Weird Tales*®, except as book reviewer. We take this opportunity to recognize and salute his many important contributions to the development of this magazine, not the least of which was the impetus to get it started in the first place. We wish him well at whatever he does in the future.

The new masthead reflects realities, George Scithers as publisher since he does most of the production work, plus such gritty slave-labor as keeping track of the money; Darrell Schweitzer as editor since he is probably the one most shaping policy these days; Carol Adams as managing editor, since, with inexpressibly deft patience and skill, she manages us, making sure things get done; Michael Betancourt (younger brother of John) as assistant, for his valued assistance, and so forth.

This does not mean that Darrell alone buys stories, which would look mighty suspicious whenever we buy one of his own. We still have a three-way balance

**Publisher:**
George H. Scithers

**Editor:**
Darrell Schweitzer

**Managing Editor:**
Carol Adams

**Assistant Editors:**
Leslie Smith, Dainis Bisenieks, Diane Weinstein, Michael W. Betancourt, & Don Keller

**Circulation Manager:**
Richard Kabakjian

**Computer Consultant:**
David J. Williams III

**Of Counsel:**
Yale F. Edeiken

**Typesetter:**
Campus Copy Center

**Printer & Soft-Cover Binder:**
Malloy Lithographing, Inc.

**Hard-Cover Binder:**
Hoster Bindery, Inc.

**Mailing:**
Unit Packaging Corporation

**Manuscript Submissions:**

Please hold all unsolicited submissions until July of 1991. After that, yes; we will read unsolicited submissions — **if** they are in standard manuscript format. Editors survive only by insisting on a few Rules: each submission must include a return envelope with your address and enough postage to bring the manuscript back to you. If it's cheaper to have us discard the manuscript if not bought, tell us so, but include a business-letter-size envelope with your address and postage so we may send you our comments. Affix postage to envelope; don't send loose stamps.

Proper manuscript format is discussed in many reference works. Some of us have even written one: *On Writing Science Fiction: the Editors Strike Back!* by Scithers, Schweitzer, & Ford; $19.50 in hardcovers, from Owlswick Press, P.O. Box 8243, Philadelphia PA 19101-8243. Another excellent work from the same publisher is Barry B. Longyear's *Science-Fiction Writer's Workshop*: $9.50 in trade paperback. These prices include shipping and handling; in Pennsylvania, please include 6% sales tax.

We cannot be responsible for manuscripts in transit or in our hands; you **must** keep a copy of every manuscript you send out, and you **must** put your name and address on the first page of every manuscript. Please: no padded envelopes, folders, or binders; and no registered or certified mail.

of power, in which George and Darrell each get a vote, and the others collectively count as one. If the story is by one of us, that one doesn't vote and the others have to be unanimous.

**What we really don't want to see in _Weird Tales_®:** In his short time here, Michael Betancourt has already developed a list of things we'd rather not see in manuscripts, beyond what _all_ editors dislike: hazy dot-matrix, fan-folded printouts, yellow crayon on orange paper, sentimental tales of truth and beauty handwritten in yak blood, and the like. We quote (or paraphrase) at length:

Fad Themes. **1)** Stories about beaten, abused children and the retribution their abusers (often) receive. We're not saying that child abuse isn't wrong and the perpetrators don't deserve retribution, but that we're tired of reading stories _about_ child abuse. **2)** The horror of pollution and what evils it might bring to light. We are all in agreement that pollution is bad. So what else is new? **3)** Swords_women_ on quests are also becoming a tired subject for us. We _are_ looking for good sword-and-sorcery fantasy, and we don't care about the gender of the quester. Making one a woman was novel when C.L. Moore was writing Jirel of Joiry for _Weird Tales_® in the '30s. It isn't new today.

All-Too-Common Themes. A routine treatment of these won't get you into print. You must do something truly original with one of these old (and a bit tired) ideas to sell the result to us: **1)** Stories without _evident_ fantastic content. It helps if the characters _believe_ something supernatural is going on. In a few cases ambiguity may help. Murkiness, however, does not. **2)** Stories in which a (usually morally rotten) person with a weak heart is given a fatal shock by some Horror conjured up for the sole purpose of placing the faint-hearted six feet under.

Wholly Unacceptable Themes. These should be given a decent burial: **1)** "And it was all a dream . . ." For decades editors have been railing against this one. It is the Cliché That Will Not Die. **2)** It is awfully difficult to do something _new_ with narrators who haven't noticed that they are dead or who die in the course of the story without explaining how they finished telling their stories. Gene Wolfe worked two variants on this one in _Weird Tales_® 290: "The Dead Man" and "The Other Dead Man," but they worked because they were _fresh_ and _original_. **3)** Stories peopled by stereotypes, such as (the all too common) dumb hillbillies and homicidal rednecks. We recall Manly Wade Wellman's observation that if, up in the hills, you actually _called_ a man a hillbilly, "he would think it his bounden duty to remove your neck from your body." These stereotypes are as bad as the dumb Irishmen, stingy Jews, and comic Darkies of old. We have no use for them. **4)** Stories in which a terror-stricken householder kills another member of the family or a friend by mistake. It _was_ shocking once upon a time, but the impact wore off long ago. **5)** Stories which "really happened." Merely telling the truth is not enough to convince our readers. There are people out there who apparently can't make something as mundane as a bus ride believable. On the other hand, if you really and truly met the South Carolina Lizard Man on your way to visit Elvis aboard a flying saucer, and it all _really happened_, there _are_ periodicals interested in your tale. They can be found at the checkout counters of most supermarkets. **6)** And we are getting tired of what you might call the mechanics of vampirism, based entirely on old movies rather than folklore. We are not looking for yet another exploration of how much sunblock lotion vampires need or whether or not they have to _lie_ in their native earth or merely carry it around with them in

Hester Lane, recently arrived in Victorian London and penniless, has discovered through a newspaper ad that she's had a change in fortune—she is an hieress, the long lost niece of a missing-and-presumed-dead doctor: Henry Jekyll.

The spine-tingling sequel to Robert Louis Stevenson's *Dr. Jekyll and Mr. Hyde,* by two of the grandest of grand masters.

Ziploc freezer bags. We *do* like vampires, and wish we could get other stories as good as Tad Williams's "Child of an Ancient City" in *Weird Tales*® 292.

New horrors are always more horrible, *because* they are *new*.

**The Lovecraft Centennial:** August 20th, 1990 marked the hundredth anniversary of the birth of our most distinguished contributor ever: Howard Phillips Lovecraft, who alone of the "pulp" writers of his generation seems well on his way to a major, world-wide critical reputation.

There were festivities in Lovecraft's native Providence last August, notably a three-day conference at Brown University for which Lovecraft scholars and fans from all over the world gathered. We regret that no *Weird Tales*® staffers were there. The one most likely to have attended — Darrell — was in Italy at the time, reputedly standing on the porch of Rome's Pantheon, hoping that, just like Martin Padway in *Lest Darkness Fall,* he would find himself miraculously transported back to antiquity. (It didn't happen. He didn't even get hit by lightning. But he does report that *modern* Italy has the best ice cream in the world, something Lovecraft would have appreciated.)

The day after the conference, a plaque to Lovecraft was unveiled in the garden adjoining Brown University's John Hay Library. On this page, you see a copy of the text and decoration of the plaque, sent to us by S.T. Joshi.

We quote from the publicity release Will Murray sent:

"The bronze plaque is a joint City of Providence, Brown University, and Friends of H.P. Lovecraft undertaking. It was formally dedicated on the one-hundredth anniversary of Lovecraft's birth, August 20, by Marilee Taylor, University Librarian at Brown, Providence Superintendent of Parks Nancy Derrick, and S.T. Joshi, who in his remarks said: 'Lovecraft in his life may have been a poor, obscure, and unappreciated genius. But we, his friends, are determined to insure that his posthumous life will be very different.'

". . . private donations came in so rapidly that press releases prepared for the fan press were not sent out because the target amount — $3,000.00 — had been reached. Approximately $6,000.00 was raised. Surplus funds will be turned over to Brown University, along with the name, Friends of H.P. Lovecraft, for the purpose of establishing a perpetual fund for the preservation, restoration, and acquisition of Lovecraft's papers and manuscripts.

"Further donations may be sent to: Friends of H.P. Lovecraft Restoration Fund, The John Hay Library, Brown University, Box A, Providence RI 02912."

We had our own Lovecraftian adventure a month earlier when the editorial We (in this case, Darrell Schweitzer) attended the Horror Writers of America awards banquet in Providence in early July and during an off three hours, with

**Howard Phillips Lovecraft**
(1890 - 1937)
**U.S. Author**

I never can be tied to raw new things,
For I first saw the light in an old town,
Where from my window huddled roofs sloped down
To a quaint harbour rich with visionings.

Streets with carved doorways where the sunset beams
Flooded old fanlights and small window-panes,
And Georgian steeples topped with gilded vanes —
These are the sights that shaped my childhood dreams

Dedicated on the Centennial of his birth
August 20, 1990
by
The City of Providence
Brown University
and
Friends of H.P. Lovecraft

9

a copy of Harry L. Beckwith's *Lovecraft's Providence* in hand, paced out the Lovecraftian Tour of College Hill, visiting two of the Old Gent's residences as well as the Charles Dexter Ward house, the St. John's Churchyard, the stump of the apple tree that ate Roger Williams, and other sites. This proved enormously useful three weeks later when We found Ourself impromptu tour-guide of a bus trip from the Northeast Regional Fantasy Convention (or NECon). You never know when you will be called upon to find the Shunned House in the dark . . .

That evening, we were also called upon to deliver a toast to Lovecraft's memory on Prospect Terrace, looking down over a sunset vista of Providence so beloved by him, and, incidentally, by his more sinister creation Charles Dexter Ward:

*A Toast, Over the Grave of Howard Phillips Lovecraft, On the Occasion of his Ninety-Ninth and Eleven-Twelfths Birthday, Delivered at NECon X, July 19, 1990:*

We are here to honor Howard Phillips Lovecraft, not because it is fifty-three years since his death and he is still remembered, or even because he would have been one hundred about this time next month, but because, in a very real sense, he has never left us.

HPL's fiction is more popular than ever, yes. But in his day, even in the pages of *Weird Tales*®, there were writers just as popular or even more so; yet nobody gathers like this over the grave of Seabury Quinn.

Lovecraft is a continuing presence. The point is not that he wrote "The Whisperer in Darkness" or "The Shadow out of Time," as substantial accomplishments as those may have been; but he is, for all of us, someone we have come to know more completely than many people we know in the flesh. We dip into his *Selected Letters*, and there he is: our brilliant, erudite,

slightly dotty, and ultimately wise acquaintance. He enters our lives in odd ways. I think all of us can remember when we first met him, and how that changed what came after. Many of us were brought into the horror field through Lovecraft, as writers or as fans. I doubt if many of us would be at NECon if it were not for H.P. Lovecraft.

We owe all manner of debt to him. He has kept words alive which certainly would have perished: squamous, rugose, and most especially *eldritch*. For any writer, he is an archetype, against whom we measure not just what we write, but how we live our lives.

He has enriched us, heightening everything from our appreciation of ice cream and cats, to our wonder at the vast and unfathomable reaches of the cosmos.

All we can say is, "Thank you, Howard. Thank you."

Noted author **John Shirley** writes from San Francisco CA:

*I read with some amusement Margaret Frastley's rather neurotic letter in the latest WT. (Isn't Margaret Frastley almost a name from an Edward Gorey poem?) Silly of her to vilify Schow. Doubtless the numerous fans of this fine writer will be outraged. As for horror writers like Schow and myself being "subversive and decadent" — well, we try!*

*Schow is actually quite a subtle writer, and he can be masterfully understated when the story calls for it. It's all a matter of expressionistic needs for a particular subtext.*

*The so-called splatterpunks are, it seems to me, protest writers; sometimes they've got a lot in common with certain painters of social commentary, like Goya. The splatterpunks make broad use of the color red in their canvasses because, in a sense, they're in their Red Period (no menstruation jokes, Schow) — it's the appropriate period of time for it. The world is a cruel and brutal place, and the splatterpunks are metaphori-*

*cally processing their world.*

*I myself worry from time to time — especially with respect to slasher films that seem to focus on violence to women — that we're desensitizing people to violence, but I think that writers like Schow are working in a realm beyond that consideration. He's writing for adults, and he's tempering it all with insight and wit and style.*

*Ms. Frastley says that the point of macabre fiction is to disturb. Well — it's quite clear that Ms. Frastley was disturbed by Schow! So Schow's stuff worked on her in accordance with her own prescription! But really, she should not be making these prescriptions. The point of macabre fiction probably changes from story to story and reader to reader. I've heard it said that we write "poetry about death" and I like that better, myself — but I'm not about to superimpose it on anyone. There's room for a wide spectrum of horror writings. Ms. Frastley, in trying to limit us to one hue, is treading the border of censorship — and that subverts what is best about America.*

**John Bracy** writes from Tempe, AZ:
*Who IS Margaret Frastley?!*

*After suffering through a severe giggle-attack at the sight of the inimical Ms. Frastley's written word (The Eyrie in #298), I lapsed into a state of utter confusion. How can an "avid horror fan (and contributor to several small press publications)"(!) never have heard of David Schow? How can anyone presumably able to read classify "Monster Movies" as subversive? The whole letter, in fact, fairly reeked of pestilential paranoia. One had to question its authenticity — or at least refer to the calendar to certify that, yes, this is indeed the year 1990 where a ripened horror scene or two really shouldn't surprise anybody. If a person wants to read Mary Poppins and Chitty-Chitty Bang-Bang, there are still a number of the more chaste comic books in print — but a professional horror magazine? What did Ms. Frastley ex-*

*pect? Her assertions that Schow's "type of writing" is "outrageously crude," etc. were absurd to say the most — easily dismissed as the over-reactive ravings of yet another xenophobic amateur writer. If the readership didn't get at least a little repulsed during their ride through* Weird Tales, *they'd resort to watching TV. I personally am not thrilled with the idea of a placebo magazine; there's enough of that going around already. As a self-described horror enthusiast, one has to ponder just what sort of material Ms. Frastley's been getting into. With the colorful language she chose to illustrate her opinions, it's difficult — if not impossible — to imagine her watching anything but slasher films.*

The Frastley letter is, we assure you, quite genuine, and printed as written. The thing that puzzles us the most is her P.S., in which she expresses approval for Darrell Schweitzer's "Soft," a story which is much more explicitly gory and not-so-subtly sexual than much of Schow — certainly much more so than "Monster Movies." We received another letter, from **Matthew Alan Cheney** of Plymouth, NH who complained that "The David J. Schow stories read like stuff that Mom and Dad said was okay to read!" In other words, that they were *much* too restrained!

To conclude this particular controversy, we got a most explicit form of reader protest from **Paul Gunning** of Ormond Beach, FL, who writes:

*Your opening statement in the Eyrie of #299 was incorrect. The most obvious wrong thing you've done is to begin to trash the grand tradition of* Weird Tales *by resorting to smut and four-letter words in the stories you publish. Your reply to Mr. O'Brien's letter is completely off the mark. What in heaven's name is meant by "We are in the post shock-effect age?" Do you ever go to the movies or turn on your television set?*

*Your reference to "profanity or ex-*

plicit sexual material" as realism is hackneyed — you either like that junk or you don't. Did you ever consider that the readers of weird fiction may not be realism freaks? Maybe they just prefer to delve for a few hours at a time into the world that is unrealistic! *The profanity and smut we can get any time. The original* Weird Tales *was truly something different and unusual. Your stated philosophy will lead it down a pedestrian road that has already become offensive.*

*I'm sure you will survive the cancellation of my subscription, but please cancel it anyhow. Adieu* WT — *parting is such sweet sorrow!*

We are always sorry to lose a reader, but there are times when 'tis a bitter pill, but good physick. We're gambling that our policies will gain us more readers than they lose. Our *Weird Tales*® must be a product of its own time, not a pastiche of the styles — and cultural values — of fifty years ago. We can only assume that Mr. Gunning finds *no* other contemporary horror to his taste, because *Weird Tales*® is — and frankly we've gotten more complaints about this than we have in the tenor of Mr. Gunning's — about the mildest on the market. Hastur forbid he should discover the Splatterpunks, or even Stephen King.

The logic here we find a bit difficult to follow. If one only reads "smut" because one "likes that junk," then does one only read a story which, incidentally, happens to have a battle scene in it because one *likes* mass-killing? Or could it be that the subject matter, inherently unpleasant in itself, serves some larger artistic end?

**Eric M. Larson** asks a question:

*The Robert E. Howard poems that* Weird Tales *has published (so far, "The Chant Demonic" and "Memories") really intrigue me. Neither are listed in Glenn Lord's 1976 book that I thought listed EVERYTHING Howard ever wrote, be it published or unpublished.*

*Perhaps I am missing something. It would be worth a note in* The Eyrie *as to 1) the origin of these poems, and 2) how they came to the attention of* Weird Tales. *I would bet there is at least one other Robert E. Howard fan out there who is wondering the same things . . .*

They came to our attention because Glenn Lord sent them to us. We can only assume that more material has been discovered since 1976. With a writer who left behind such vast and messy literary remains as Howard, this is extremely likely. After all, a *whole book* of Howard's poetry turned up in the papers of Howard's friend Tevis Clyde Smith and was recently published by Donald Grant as *Shadows of Dreams*.

The technical term we editors use for what follows is "a blithering idiot letter." We print it to warn others away from such follies. **Disgusted**, who has had stories returned to him unread, writes from San Francisco:

Weird Tales *will obviously fold. Your nitpicking rules about manuscript submissions has just lost you some excellent work by topnotch writers. Clearly typed single-space isn't good enough for you? Computer word count isn't good enough for you? Maybe if you hired some* real *editors you wouldn't need to stress* FORM *over* CONTENT! *Nobody minds resubmitting double-space after* acceptance!

To which we can reply, well, gee, if we've lost some top-notch writers this way, we will just have to make do with those like Stephen King, Robert Bloch, William F. Nolan, Ramsey Campbell, and Jonathan Carroll, all of whom deign to type double-spaced the first time around.

**Robert Grano** writes from Coraopolis PA:

*Thanks for the Chet Williamson issue. I've been a fan of his for several years, catching many of his fine stories in F&SF. The interview with him was very interesting, especially the bit about* whether it's important or necessary to believe (or disbelieve) in what you're writing about. You were correct to point out that some skepticism on the reader's part is necessary. But on the other hand, you can't forget that many great writers of the supernatural believed strongly in the supernatural themselves — M.R. James, Charles Williams, and Russell Kirk come to mind. Of course if the writer incorporates too many of his or her own beliefs about the supernatural into the story, the story will most likely fail, as many of Conan Doyle's did after he became an ardent spiritualist.

This same problem can be seen in the work of the bestselling Christian author Frank Peretti. Peretti has been compared to Stephen King and C.S. Lewis by various Christian reviewers, but these comparisons are invalid because Peretti isn't really a fantasist. His fiction, which concerns angels, demons, occultism, etc., fails for the most part because he himself believes what he's writing — to him it's not fantasy, it's reality. It may be speculative, but only slightly.

I can also see this problem surfacing in my own reading of horror stories. My parents are exorcists (in Christian circles this practice is known as "deliverance ministry"), and have been since I was nine or ten. I've heard, seen, and been told about a lot of strange things in the ensuing twenty years. Consequently, I have absolutely no interest in any stories that deal with demon possession. That subject holds no fear for me. I guess you could say I got used to hearing deep, masculine voices come out of young women! Anyway, these show just how complex the belief/disbelief problem is.

Our own feeling is that fantasy, as opposed to religious literature or mythology, contains an element which is deliberately, consciously *made up*. We can only quote H.P. Lovecraft's *Super-*

*natural Horror In Literature*: "It may be well to remark here that occult believers are probably less effective than materialists in delineating the spectral and fantastic, since to them the phantom world is so commonplace a reality that they tend to refer to it with less awe, remoteness, and impressiveness than do those who see it as an absolute and stupendous violation of the natural order."

**Herbert Anthony Kauderer** comments on the discussion of poetry in #298:

*I believe that poetry as an art form has knocked down every barrier restricting its freedom. This is by itself a fine thing. I believe that poetry is a medium through which anything should be possible. . . . Total freedom implies many things. It implies the freedom to write sonnets, alliterative verse, or free verse as you choose. You can write in images so personal that no one else can understand what you're saying, or in images so universal that anyone literate enough to read the poem will be touched. . . . The problem, in my mind, is that the poets have convinced everyone that they* should *be completely obscure. In the course of obtaining my B.A. (cum laude) in English, I had to continually fight for my right to be lucid. This doesn't mean that I can't occasionally write obscure poetry. Hell, I've sold poems that couldn't mean to anyone else what they mean to me.*

*I believe that modern poetry needs more magazines that set their own standards instead of adhering to financially destructive literary conventions. If* Weird Tales *decided to use only formal verse that would not curb the freedom of poetry as an artform. It would merely change the standards of one small but valuable corner of the poetry market.*

We can only suspect that the "obscure" poems you sold were published not on the strength of what they meant to you, then, but on what they meant to others, however coincidentally. Unless you are truly writing for an audience of one,

poetry is as public an art form as any other. It must serve its audience. The "financially destructive" convention you refer to is simply the idea that it can discard the audience. Fine, but the audience can discard the poetry too — and has.

Poet **Walter Shedlofsky** sends us some further notes on this subject:

*I agree with your statement on the malaise in poetry, not specifically in fantastic verse. I believe this can be attributed to the fact that there is no incentive to write poetry, let alone quality verse. The poetic market is practically non-existent and the compensation is atrociously minimal. Too often the only compensation is seeing the verse in print.*

That, yes, but more. There may be no incentive, but many people are still trying to write what they imagine to be poetry. We think the more serious problems are 1) collapse of standards due to academic influence and 2) loss of an audience willing to believe there is any contemporary poetry worth reading. Even if the standards can be raised, it's still going to be a while before readers can be coaxed back.

**The Most Popular Story:** The clear winner for *Weird Tales*® 298 was "The Unmaker of Men" by Darrell Schweitzer and Jason Van Hollander. Not too far behind that was "Jabbie Welsh" by Chet Williamson. Third place went to "1/72nd Scale" by Ian MacLeod, an unusually strong showing for a brand-new writer. This was Mr. MacLeod's first weird story, and his first story published in America. He had previously published in Britain, in *Interzone*, and now he seems to be everywhere, such as on the cover of the Mid-December, 1990, issue of *Isaac Asimov's Science Fiction Magazine*. "Ember" by Fred Chappell and "Heart's Desire" by Chet Williamson also drew many favorable comments.

Ω

# THE DEN

by John Gregory Betancourt

**Revolution! Change! Old ideas overthrown!**

A revolution (albeit a quiet one) has come to horror publishing. You won't hear much about it, and most readers won't care one whit, but it's there and it's quite important. To be more specific: desktop publishing.

*Weird Tales®* is desktop-published. Pages are produced in the *WT* offices on an MS-DOS computer (an Everex 1800) a word-processing program (XyWrite, from XyQuest), and a typesetting program (Ventura, from Xerox), and then printed oversize on a Model 4045 laser printer (also from Xerox).

Why? Because it saves time, which means less inventory and less last-minute panics. It makes publishing *Weird Tales®* far more cost-effective than it would otherwise be. There is a lesson to be learned: if the *Weird Tales®* staff can produce a professional magazine on home computers (and a thoroughly first-class outside company to do the actual printing and binding), other people can, too.

In fact, they are already doing so. Quietly, desktop publishing has snuck into the horror field and taken over.

Since last issue, I've received two new horror magazines worth noting. Both have full-color covers. Both are produced on office computers. They are: *Cemetery Dance* (4 issues/$15.00 from PO Box 858, Englewood, MD 21040 — make checks payable to Richard T. Chizmar) and *Iniquities: The Magazine of Great Wickedness and Wonder* (4 issues/$19.95 from: 167 N. Sierra Bonita Ave., Pasadena, CA 91106). Both have design problems, however, which I expect will be overcome in future issues.

*Iniquities* shows what can go wrong when people get too enthusiastic with a MacIntosh computer's layout and design possibilities; it's vastly over-produced, and the type quality is less than appealing because the print-out is too grainy. The contributors (Clive Barker, David J. Schow, John Skipp, Somtow Sucharitkul, Richard Matheson, Tim Sullivan, etc.) are all terrific. Too much of the material is reprinted or excerpted, however. This issue was much delayed, so expect difficulties in *Iniquities* keeping to any sort of regular production schedule.

*Cemetery Dance* has a generally clean layout, but the publisher hasn't figured out how to make the quotation marks work. One problem: some of the pages look a little too computer-generated. It doesn't stop *Cemetery Dance* from being quite a lot of fun; the issue I have is volume 2, number 4 (Fall 1990), a "J.N. Williamson Special," with work by Williamson and a number of authors familiar from the small press. Its greatest strength seems to be its non- fiction, with plenty of columns, profiles, interviews, and reviews.

The production problems with both magazines are minor and, with a little work, can be overcome. Both are worth watching for.

Desktop publishing has become so affordable (as publishing goes) that I wouldn't be surprised to look up and suddenly find five or six new horror magazines with full color covers, typeset interiors, and professional contents being published . . . not by professional publishing companies, but by entrepreneurial fans. And not in ten years, but tomorrow.

What about books? The phenomenon is certainly spreading there as well. *Cold Chills* (reviewed a couple of issues ago) is one example: an oddly bound hardcover horror anthology, produced on a home computer, printed (I imagine) at a local copy store, then bound at a local bindery.

George Scithers's private publishing company, Owlswick Press (to cite one example I know well), has long produced beautiful hardcover books. Anyone who has seen the elegant Owlswick editions of Lord Dunsany's fantasy stories knows what I mean: George doesn't skimp on quality. Using his office computers, these days he's producing books faster, more economically, and just as elegantly as ever. (The same goes for the Weird Tales Library imprint, which George and Darrell work on for Terminus. Same computers: same production values.) Check out any of the Owlswick or Weird Tales Library books to see what I mean.

And of course I also have my own anecdote to tell. It seems I've become involved in starting up my own publishing company, which I've named Wildside Press. How did this happen? That's a story! (Those bored by long-winded publishing tales may now skip ahead to the reviews.)

### Still here? Good.

Once, long ago, I was vice president of the Philadelphia Science Fiction Society. PSFS had selected Fritz Leiber as Principal Speaker at their 1990 Conference, Philcon. I had this bright idea — why not publish a collection of Fritz Leiber's essays to commemorate the event?

Everyone in PSFS agreed it would be a good idea, so I agreed to get printing estimates, find out if Leiber would let us have the rights to his essays, etc. etc.

By the time I got back to PSFS with my estimates, we had about four months to go until the convention. Everyone agreed the book was still a good idea. Only nobody believed I could produce the book in four months.

I told them I could. I explained how. (One month to keyboard the book into the computer, one month to typeset the pages and get the layout right, one month to print and bind: it's a three month process using desktop publishing techniques. I had my own computer; I had my own laser printer. I could do it. Really. Truly. Honest!)

They still didn't believe me. They wouldn't agree to let me produce the book for them.

I felt immensely frustrated; I'd even (based on their enthusiastic support earlier) negotiated the contract with Fritz Leiber's agent. What to do? The only answer, it seemed, was to publish the book myself.

I did so. In three months. I not only had copies at Philcon, but at the World Fantasy Convention two weeks earlier.

I cut a lot of corners, I admit. I didn't have a professional typesetting program, so I used WordPerfect, a word processor, and it came close. Because of

**17**

the rush there are more typos in the book than there should be†, and the printer misled me about what margins would look best. But overall I'm happy with the book. I think it's a terrific first effort, and very satisfying because I not only proved a point with it, but I did it entirely on my own.

And I discovered I like publishing books. I bought a professional typesetting program, upgraded my laser printer, and contracted to publish six more: three novels by Robert Weinberg, (including *The Armageddon Box*, the sequel to *The Devil's Auction*, the first Weird Tales Library book), and short story collections by Mike Resnick, Alan Rodgers, and Nina Kiriki Hoffman.

By the time you read this, Weinberg's *The Armageddon Box* and Resnick's *Pink Elephants and Hairy Toads* will be out. Do my wife (Kim) a favor and pick up copies — she's quite nervous about all this publishing stuff, and I'd like to prove her wrong, too!

**On to the reviews:**

*At the Mountains of Madness*, by H.P. Lovecraft. Donald M. Grant, 95 pp., $125.00 (hc)
*Lovecraft's Legacy*, edited by Robert Weinberg and Martin H. Greenberg. TOR Books, 320 pp., $18.95 (hc)

In 1990 we celebrated Lovecraft's 100th birthday. Two books in particular stand out: first, Donald M. Grant's absolutely stunning edition of "At the Mountains of Madness." Donald M. Grant has taken Lovecraft's novella and produced one of the most beautiful books of 1990. It measures approximately 13.5 inches by 9.5, bound on the 9.5-inch side. The binding is leather and smells terrific. (I have a fondness for leather books.) It includes 15 color plates (with a total of more than 50 individual illustrations) by a Brazilian artist I've never heard of, Fernando Duval, who does a marvellous job of capturing the feel of that period.

The introduction is by Les Daniels. All copies are signed by Fernando Duval. Contrary to the printing information in the book, only 875 copies were actually produced, instead of the stated 1,000 copies. I'm not sure if it's still in print, but the publisher still had copies at the World Fantasy Convention in October, 1990. Write and ask: Donald M. Grant Publisher, Inc., P.O. Box 187, Hampton Falls NH 03844.

*Lovecraft's Legacy*, on the other hand, is an attempt by contemporary authors to pay homage to Lovecraft's continued influence. (What horror writer hasn't been influenced by Lovecraft in some way — whether open pastiches of his Cthulhu Mythos stories, or more subtly through the techniques Lovecraft used to scare the socks off readers?) Among the authors who contribute stories are Gene Wolfe, Graham Masterton, Gahan Wilson, and F. Paul Wilson.

As I understand it, Wilson's story would have formed the core of a special F. Paul Wilson issue of *Weird Tales®* (it's Cthulhu Mythos), only the editors of this anthology talked him into letting them have it. (Grrr!) The stories are (as usual with such tributes) a mixed bag; but enough stand out to make it worthwhile.

*The Brains of Rats*, by Michael Blumlein, Scream/Press, 224 pp., $25.00
A friend of mine has been raving about Blumlein's work for the last six months. I finally had enough of it, and sat down with *The Brains of Rats* — Blumlein's short story collection — to see what all the excitement's about.

Blumlein writes the strangest, most disturbing fiction I have ever found. He defies placement within the horror genre because his stories are *sui generis*. There is, literally, nothing like them

---

† Good proofreading *always* takes more time and effort than one thought it would. – GHS

being published anywhere in the field.

Blumlein uses experimental techniques, odd voices, strange asides to the reader, morbid lumps of lecture, and a fascination with sex and icky medical things to weave a series of stories so intense, so morbidly fascinating, that I literally could not stop reading. And sometimes I really wanted to stop: Blumlein's stories are unpleasant glimpses into an insane inner world where dream-logic holds sway. To attempt to describe them is, to some extent, an exercise in futility; how can you describe something which is so unique it's impossible to draw parallels?

I searched (in vain) for a passage to quote which would sum up my reading experience. Taken out of context, quotes didn't quite seem to work with Blumlein. You'll just have to trust me; if you're adventurous, have a strong stomach, and want one of the darkest rides of your life, get a copy. Order from: Scream/Press, PO Box 481146, Los Angeles CA 90048. Add $2.00 for postage & handling.

*Sleepwalker,* by Michael Cadnum.
St. Martin's Press, 224 pp., $5.95 (hc)

My father is an archaeologist (specializing in Minoan Greece), so stories with an archaeological setting have always interested me. Cadnum's novel is set at an excavation of Anglo-Saxon artifacts in Yorkshire, England. The usual mysterious happenings happen: tools are missing, freak accidents disturb the local workers, coffee cups and other articles rearrange themselves in locked rooms during the night.

Our archaeologist-hero is a studious scientist plagued by sleep-walking since his wife's death. He comes to York in search of therapy through hard work. But when the preserved body of a murdered Anglo-Saxon king turns up in the peat, superstitious workmen know it's part of a curse.

Or is it? Cadnum weaves a fine thriller, tipping the reader's expecta-

tions — are the odd doings supernatural or man-made? — first one way, then the other. The archaeological parts of the book are quite believable and well done; I enjoyed it.

*Screams: Three Novels of Suspense,* by Robert Bloch. Underwood-Miller, 542 pp., $39.95 (hc)

The latest trend seems to be toward huge volumes collecting much of an author's work: witness the mammoth groupings of short stories by Philip K. Dick, Richard Matheson, Robert Sheckley, and several others over the last decade. It's a good idea because so much work is otherwise unavailable.

*Screams* collects (for first hardcover publication) three of Bloch's suspense novels: *Firebug, The Star Stalker,* and *The Will to Kill.* Bloch is not only a current master of the horror genre, but a seminal influence on the field. No collection complete without, and so on.

This collection goes right on the shelf with the others.

Order from: Underwood-Miller, 708 Westover Dr., Lancaster PA 17601. Ask for a catalog; they do a lot of books worth owning.

**In short:**

*Fire,* by Alan Rodgers (Bantam, $4.95 {pb}) was a modest best-seller; it's an end-of-the-world potboiler, mixing evil religious fanaticism with a virus that reconstructs the dead from any remnant of DNA. Although it borrows too heavily from Robert McCammon's *Swan Song,* and doesn't have enough to say to support its length, these problems are minor so early in a developing writer's career (this is Rodgers's second novel, and quite remarkable *as* a second novel). While not Literature, *Fire* is entertaining and worth seeking out. Rodgers has length and style down pat; with more practice, when grasp and reach mesh more closely, he'll join the big ones in the horror field.

**News & gossip & house ads & such:**

Stuart Schiff reports that he's assembling a new issue of *Whispers. Whispers* may well be the finest horror magazine published in the last 20 years (not counting *WT,* of course). I will duly report all details.

*Pulphouse: The Hardback Magazine* is about to stop publication. It's not the end, though — the ever-enterprising Pulphouse Publishing crew is planning to launch a *weekly* (yes, weekly) science fiction/fantasy/horror magazine under the *Pulphouse* title. If anyone can pull off a weekly magazine, it'll be them, although I have my doubts. I certainly wish Dean Wesley Smith (publisher) and Kris Rusch (editor) all success.

Owlswick Press has three new books out: *Anita,* by Keith Roberts; *The Infinite Kingdoms,* by Michael Rutherford; and *The Adventures of Doctor Eszterhazy* by Avram Davidson. All three authors have had work in *Weird Tales®* recently. Get 'em while they're hot.

Wildside Press, my own personal imprint (see the introductory essay) will also have three new books out by the time you read this. The first is *Fafhrd & Me: Selected Essays,* by Fritz Leiber (200-copy hardcover edition: $25.00; trade paperback: $9.95); *Pink Elephants and Hairy Toads,* by Mike Resnick, a collection of humorous fantasy stories (250-copy hardcover, signed by Resnick, Martha Soukup {the introduction}, Pat Cadigan {the afterword}, and Rob Alexander {the artist}: $25.00); and *The Armageddon Box,* by Robert Weinberg (400-copy numbered, boxed edition, signed by Weinberg and artist Stephen Fabian: $35.00). *The Armageddon Box* is the sequel to *The Devil's Auction,* and it's even better, in my opinion. Hey, but what do I know? I'm trying to sell you the book. Order from: John Betancourt, 37 Fillmore St., Newark NJ 07105. Make checks payable to my wife, Kim Betancourt.

**Review copies:**

All review copies should be sent to my home address above. Chatty letters are nice, too.                    Ω

---

# WEIRD TALES, THE MAGAZINE THAT NEVER DIES

## by Marvin Kaye

When I was a child growing up in West Philadelphia, two factors shaped my early interest in the bizarre and supernatural. The first was the local motion picture theatre across the street. The other was the frequent presence in our household of a magazine with lurid covers and ominously-titled contents: *Weird Tales*.

Two issues of "The Unique Magazine" especially loom in my memory. Before them, I never finished reading anything I started, but in March 1947 and again in September of that same year, I could not stop reading three "Weird Tales," word for word. For the record, then, my literacy began with August Derleth's ghostly "Mr. George"; C. Hall Thompson's ghastly "The Pale Criminal"; and Manly Banister's poignant lycanthropic romance, "Eena." I repaid my debt to them by including them in my Doubleday Science Fiction Book Club anthology, *Weird Tales, the Magazine That Never Dies*.

Back in the forties, few members of the respectable literary establishment (so-called) thought much of pulp magazines, but nowadays the myopic academics have finally realized what we've all known most of our lives: that *Weird Tales* was *AND STILL IS* the most important periodical devoted to imaginative fiction in the history of American literature. No other serial publication, not even the venerable, excellent *Magazine of Fantasy and Science Fiction* has so consistently attracted, nurtured and developed such an impressive stable of writers.                                 Ω

# BEETLES

## by Robert Bloch

When Hartley returned from Egypt, his friends said he had changed. The specific nature of that change was difficult to detect, for none of his acquaintances got more than a casual glimpse of him. He dropped around to the club just once, and then retired to the seclusion of his apartment. His manner was so definitely hostile, so markedly anti-social, that very few of his cronies cared to visit him, and the occasional callers were not received.

It caused considerable talk at the time — gossip rather. Those who remembered Arthur Hartley in the days before his expedition abroad were naturally quite cut up over the drastic metamorphosis in his manner. Hartley had been known as a keen scholar, a singularly erudite field-worker in his chosen profession of archeology; but at the same time he had been a peculiarly charming person. He had the worldly flair usually associated with the fictional characters of E. Phillips Oppenheim, and a positively devilish sense of humor which mocked and belittled it. He was the kind of fellow who could order the precise wine at the proper moment, at the same time grinning as though he were as much surprised by it all as his guest of the evening. And most of his friends found this air of culture without ostentation quite engaging. He had carried this urbane sense of the ridiculous over into his work; and while it was known that he was very much interested in archeology, and a notable figure in the field, he inevitably referred to his studies as "pottering around with old fossils and the old fossils that discovered them."

Consequently, his curious reversal following his trip came as a complete surprise.

All that was definitely known was that he had spent some eight months on a field trip to the Egyptian Sudan. Upon his return he had immediately severed all connections with the institute he had been associated with. Just what had occurred during the expedition was a matter of excited conjecture among his former intimates. But something had definitely happened; it was unmistakable.

The night he spent at the club proved that. He had come in quietly, too quietly. Hartley was one of those persons who usually made an entrance, in the true sense of the word. His tall, graceful figure, attired in the immaculate evening dress so seldom found outside of the pages of melodramatic fiction; his truly leonine head with its Stokowski-like bristle of gray hair; these attributes commanded attention. He could have passed anywhere as a man of the world, or a stage magician awaiting his cue to step onto the platform.

But this evening he entered quietly, unobtrusively. He wore dinner clothes, but his shoulders sagged, and the spring was gone from his walk. His hair was grayer, and it hung pallidly over his tanned forehead. Despite the bronze of Egyptian sun on his features, there was a sickly tinge to his countenance. His eyes peered mistily from amidst unsightly folds. His face seemed to have lost its mold; the mouth hung loosely.

He greeted no one; and took a table alone. Of course cronies came up and chatted, but he did not invite them to join him. And oddly enough, none of them insisted, although normally they would

gladly have forced their company upon him and jollied him out of a black mood, which experience had taught them was easily done in his case. Nevertheless, after a few words with Hartley, they all turned away.

They must have felt it even then. Some of them hazarded the opinion that Hartley was still suffering from some form of fever contracted in Egypt, but I do not think they believed this in their hearts. From their shocked descriptions of the man they seemed one and all to sense the peculiar *alien* quality about him. This was an Arthur Hartley they had never known, an aged stranger, with a querulous voice which rose in suspicion when he was questioned about his journey. Stranger he truly was, for he did not even appear to recognize some of the men who greeted him, and when he did it was with an abstracted manner — a clumsy way of wording it, but what else is there to say when an old friend stares blankly into silence upon meeting, and his eyes seem to fasten on far-off terrors that affright him?

That was the strangeness they all grasped in Hartley. He was afraid. Fear bestrode those sagging shoulders. Fear breathed a pallor into that ashy face. Fear grinned into those empty, far-fixed eyes. Fear prompted the suspicion in the voice.

They told me, and that is why I went round to see Arthur Hartley in his rooms. Others had spoken of their efforts, in the week following his appearance at the club, to gain admittance to his apartment. They said he did not answer the bell, and complained that the phone had been disconnected. But that, I reasoned, was fear's work.

I wouldn't let Hartley down. I had been a rather good friend of his — and I may as well confess that I scented a mystery here. The combination proved irresistible. I went up to his flat one afternoon and rang.

No answer. I went into the dim hallway

and listened for footsteps, some sign of life from within. No answer. Complete, utter silence. For a moment I thought crazily of suicide, then laughed the dread away. It was absurd — and still, there had been a certain dismaying unanimity in all the reports I had heard of Hartley's mental state. When the stolidest, most hard-headed of the club bores concurred with their estimate of the man's condition, I might well worry. Still, suicide . . .

I rang again, more as a gesture than in expectation of tangible results, and then I turned and descended the stairs. I felt, I recall, a little twinge of inexplicable relief upon leaving the place. The thought of suicide in that gloomy hallway had not been pleasant.

I reached the lower door and opened it, and a familiar figure scurried past me on the landing. I turned. It was Hartley.

For the first time since his return I got a look at the man, and in the hallway shadows he was ghastly. Whatever his condition at the club, a week must have accentuated it tremendously. His head was lowered, and as I greeted him he looked up. His eyes gave me a terrific shock. There was a stranger dwelling in their depths — a haunted stranger. I swear he shook when I addressed him.

He was wearing a tattered topcoat, but it hung loosely over his gauntness. I noticed that he was carrying a large bundle done up in brown paper.

I said something. I don't remember what; at any rate, I was at some pains to conceal my confusion as I greeted him. I was rather insistently cordial, I believe, for I could see that he would just as soon have hurried up the stairs without even speaking to me. The astonishment I felt converted itself into heartiness. Rather reluctantly he invited me up.

We entered the flat, and I noticed that Hartley double-locked the door behind him. That, to me, characterized his metamorphosis. In the old days, Hartley had always kept open house, in the literal sense of the word. Studies might have kept him late at the institute, but a chance visitor found his door open wide. And now, he double-locked it.

I turned around and surveyed the apartment. Just what I expected to see I cannot say, but certainly my mind was prepared for some sign of radical alteration. There was none. The furniture had not been moved; the pictures hung in their original places; the vast bookcases still stood in the shadows.

Hartley excused himself, entered the bedroom, and presently emerged after discarding his topcoat. Before he sat down he walked over to the mantel and struck a match before a little bronze figurine of Horus. A second later the thick gray spirals of smoke arose in the approved style of exotic fiction, and I smelt the pungent tang of strong incense.

That was the first puzzler. I had unconsciously adopted the attitude of a detective looking for clues — or, perhaps, a psychiatrist ferreting out psychoneurotic tendencies. And the incense was definitely alien to the Arthur Hartley I knew.

"Clears away the smell," he remarked.

I didn't ask "What smell?" Nor did I begin to question him as to his trip, his inexpliable conduct in not answering my correspondence after he left Khartoum, or his avoidance of my company in this week following his return. Instead, I let him talk.

He said nothing at first. His conversation rambled, and behind it all I sensed the abstraction I had been warned about. He spoke of having given up his work, and hinted that he might leave the city shortly and go up to his family home in the country. He had been ill. He was disappointed in Egyptology, and its limitations. He hated darkness. The locust plagues had increased in Kansas.

This rambling was — insane.

I knew it then, and I hugged the thought to me in the perverse delight which is born of dread. Hartley was mad. "Limitations" of Egyptology. "I hate the dark." "The locusts of Kansas."

But I sat silently when he lighted the great candles about the room; sat silently staring through the incense clouds to where the flaming tapers illuminated his twitching features. And then he broke.

"You are my friend?" he said. There was a question in his voice, a puzzled suspicion in his words that brought sudden pity to me. His derangement was terrible to witness. Still, I nodded gravely.

"You are my friend," he continued. This time the words were a statement. The deep breath which followed betokened resolution on his part.

"Do you know what was in that bundle I brought in?" he asked suddenly.

"No."

"I'll tell you. Insecticide. That's what it was. Insecticide!"

His eyes flamed in triumph which stabbed me.

"I haven't left this house for a week. I dare not spread the plague. They follow me, you know. But today I thought of the way — absurdly simple, too. I went out and bought insecticide. Pounds of it. And liquid spray. Special formula stuff, more deadly than arsenic. Just elementary science, really — but its very prosaicness may defeat the Powers of Evil."

I nodded like a fool, wondering whether I could arrange for him to be taken away that evening. Perhaps my friend, Doctor Sherman, might diagnose. . . .

"Now let them come! It's my last chance — the incense doesn't work, and even if I keep the lights burning they creep about the corners. Funny the woodwork holds up; it should be riddled."

What was this?

"But I forgot," said Hartley. "You don't know about it. The plague, I mean. And the curse." He leaned forward and his white hands made octopus-shadows on the wall.

"I used to laugh at it, you know." he said. "Archeology isn't exactly a pursuit for the superstitious. Too much groveling in ruins. And putting curses on old pottery and battered statues never seemed important to me. But Egyptology — that's different. It's human bodies, there. Mummified, but still human. And the Egyptians were a great race — they had scientific secrets we haven't yet fathomed, and of course we cannot even begin to approach their concepts in mysticism."

Ah! There was the key! I listened, intently.

"I learned a lot, this last trip. We were after the excavation job in the new tombs up the river. I brushed up on the dynastic periods, and naturally the religious significance entered into it. Oh, I know all the myths — the Bubastis legend, the Isis resurrection theory, the true names of Ra, the allegory of Set —

"We found things there, in the tombs — wonderful things. The pottery, the furniture, the bas-reliefs we were able to remove. But the expeditionary reports will be out soon; you can read of it then. We found mummies, too. Cursed mummies."

Now I saw it, or thought I did.

"And I was a fool. I did something I never should have dared to do — for ethical reasons, and for other, more important reasons. Reasons that may cost me my soul."

I had to keep my grip on myself, remember that he was mad, remember that his convincing tones were prompted by the delusions of insanity. Or else, in that dark room I might have easily believed that there was a power which had driven my friend to this haggard brink.

"Yes, I did it, I tell you! I read the Curse of Scarabæus — sacred beetle, you know — and I did it anyway. I couldn't guess that it was true. I was a skeptic; everyone is skeptical enough until things happen. Those things are like the phenomenon of death; you read about it, realize that it occurs to others, and yet

cannot quite conceive of it happening to yourself. And yet it does. The Curse of the Scarabæus was like that."

Thoughts of the Sacred Beetle of Egypt crossed my mind. And I remembered, also, the seven plagues. And I knew what he would say. . . .

"We came back. On the ship I noticed them. They crawled out of the corners every night. When I turned the light on they went away, but they always returned when I tried to sleep. I burned incense to keep them off, and then I moved into a new cabin. But they followed me.

"I did not dare tell anyone. Most of the chaps would have laughed, and the Egyptologists in the party wouldn't have helped much. Besides, I couldn't confess my crime. So I went on alone."

His voice was a dry whisper.

"It was pure hell. One night on the boat I saw the black things crawling in my food. After tht I ate in the cabin, alone. I dared not see anyone now, for fear they might notice how the things followed me. They did follow me, you know — if I walked in shadow on the deck they crept along behind. Only the sun kept them back, or a pure flame. I nearly went mad trying to account logically for their presence; trying to imagine how they got on the boat. But all the time I knew in my heart what the truth was. They were a sending — the Curse!

"When I reached port I went up and resigned. When my guilt was discovered there would have been a scandal, anyway, so I resigned. I couldn't hope to continue work with those things crawling all over, wherever I went. I was afraid to look anyone up. Naturally, I tried. That one night at the club was ghastly, though — I could see them marching across the carpet and crawling up the sides of my chair, and it took all there was in me to keep from screaming and dashing out.

"Since then I've stayed here, alone. Before I decide on any course for the future, I must fight the Curse and win. Nothing else will help."

I started to interject a phrase, but he brushed it aside and continued desperately.

"No, I couldn't go away. They followed me across the ocean; they haunt me in the streets. I could be locked up and they would still come. They come every night and crawl up the sides of my bed and try to get at my face and I must sleep soon or I'll go mad, they crawl over my face at night, they crawl —"

It was horrible to see the words ooze out between his set teeth, for he was fighting madly to control himself.

"Perhaps the insecticide will kill them. It was the first thing I should have thought of, but of course panic confused me. Yes, I put my trust in the insecticide. Grotesque, isn't it? Fighting an ancient curse with insect-powder?"

I spoke at last. "They're beetles, aren't they?"

He nodded. "Scarabæus beetles. You know the curse. The mummies under the protection of the Scarab cannot be violated."

I knew the curse. It was one of the oldest known to history. Like all legends, it had a persistent life. Perhaps I could reason.

"But why should it affect you?" I asked. Yes, I would reason with Hartley. Egyptian fever had deranged him, ad the colorful curse story had gripped his mind. If I spoke logically, I might get him to understand his hallucination. "Why should it affect you?" I repeated.

He was silent for a moment before he spoke, and then his words seemed to be wrung out of him.

"I stole a mummy," he said. "I stole the mummy of a temple virgin. I must have been crazy to do it; something happens to you under that sun. There was gold in the case, and jewels, and ornaments. And there was the Curse, written. I got them — both."

I stared at him, and knew that in this

he spoke the truth.

"That's why I cannot keep up my work. I stole the mummy, and I am cursed. I didn't believe, but the crawling things came just as the inscription said.

"At first I thought that was the meaning of the Curse, that wherever I went the beetles would go, too, that they would haunt me and keep me from men forever. But lately I am beginning to think differently. I think the beetles will act as messengers of vengeance. I think they mean to kill me."

This was pure raving.

"I haven't dared open the mummy-case since. I'm afraid to read the inscription again. I have it here in the house, but I've locked it up and I won't show you. I want to burn it — but I must keep it on hand. In a way, it's the only proof of my sanity. And if the things kill me —"

"Snap out of it," I commanded. Then I started. I don't know the exact words I used, but I said reassuring, hearty, wholesome things. And when I finished he smiled the martyred smile of the obsessed.

"Delusions? They're real. But where do they come from? I can't find any cracks in the woodwork. The walls are sound. And yet every night the beetles come and crawl up the bed and try to get at my face. They don't bite, they merely crawl. There are thousands of them — black thousands of silent, crawling things, inches long. I brush them away, but when I fall asleep they come back; they're clever, and I can't pretend. I've never caught one; they're too fast- moving. They seem to understand me — or the Power that sends them understands.

"They crawl up from Hell night after night, and I can't last much longer. Some evening I'll fall completely asleep and they will creep over my face, and then —"

He leaped to his feet and screamed.

"The corner — in the corner now — out of the walls —"

The black shadows were moving,

marching.

I saw a blur, fancied I could detect rustling forms advancing, creeping, spreading before the light.

Hartley sobbed.

I turned on the electric light. There was, of course, nothing there. I didn't say a word, but left abruptly. Hartley continued to sit huddled in his chair, his head in his hands.

I went straight to my friend, Doctor Sherman.

He diagnosed it as I thought he would: phobia, accompanied by hallucinations. Hartley's feeling of guilt over stealing the mummy haunted him. The visions of beetles resulted.

All this Sherman studded with the mumbo-jumbo technicalities of the professional psychiatrist, but it was simple enough. Together we phoned the institute where Hartley had worked. They verified the story, in so far as they knew. Hartley had stolen a mummy.

After dinner Sherman had an appointment, but he promised to meet me at ten and go with me again to Hartley's apartment. I was quite insistent about this, for I felt that there was no time to lose. Of course, this was a mawkish attitude on my part, but that strange afternoon session had deeply disturbed me.

I spent the early evening in unnerving reflection. Perhaps that was the way all so-called "Egyptian curses" worked. A guilty conscience on the part of a tomb-looter made him project the shadow of imaginary punishment on himself. He had hallucinations of retribution. That might explain the mysterious Tut-ankh-ahmen deaths; it certainly accounted for the suicides.

And that was why I insisted on Sherman seeing Hartley that same night. I feared suicide very much, for if ever a man was on the verge of complete mental collapse, Arthur Hartley surely was.

It was nearly eleven, however, before Sherman and I rang the bell. There was no answer. We stood in the dark hallway as I vainly rapped, then pounded. The silence only served to augment my anxiety. I was truly afraid, or else I never would have dared using my skeleton key.

As it was, I felt the end justified the means. We entered.

The living-room was bare of occupants. Nothing had changed since the afternoon — I could see that quite clearly, for all the lights were on, and the guttering candle-stumps still smoldered.

Both Sherman and I smelt the reek of the insecticide quite strongly, and the floor was almost evenly coated with thick white insect powder.

We called, of course, before I ventured to enter the bedroom. It was dark, and I thought it was empty until I turned on the lights and saw the figure huddled beneath the bed-clothes. It was Arthur Hartley, and I needed no second glance to see that his white face was twisted in death.

The reek of insecticide was strongest here, and incense burned; and yet there was another pungent smell — a musty odor, vaguely animal-like.

Sherman stood at my side, staring.

"What shall we do?" I asked.

"I'll get the police on the wire downstairs," he said. "Touch nothing."

He dashed out, and I followed him from the room, sickened. I could not bear to approach the body of my friend — that hideous expression on the face affrighted me. Suicide, murder, heart-attack — I didn't even wish to know the manner of his passing. I was heartsick to think that we had been too late.

I turned from the bedroom and then that damnable scent came to my nostrils redoubled, and I knew. "Beetles!"

But how could there be beetles? It was an illusion in poor Hartley's brain. Even his twisted mind had realized that there were no apertures in the walls to admit them; that they could not be seen about the place.

And still the smell rose on the air —

the odor of death, of decay, of ancient corruption that reigned in Egypt. I followed the scent to the second bedroom, forced the door.

On the bed lay the mummy-case. Hartley had said he locked it up in here. The lid was closed, but ajar.

I opened it. The sides bore inscriptions, and one of them may have pertained to the Scàrabæus Curse. I do not know, for I stared only at the ghastly, unshrouded figure that lay within. It was a mummy, and it had been sucked dry. It was all shell. There was a great cavity in the stomach, and as I peered within I could see a few feebly-crawling forms — inch-long, black buttons with great writhing feelers. They shrank back in the light, but not before I saw the scarab patterns on the outer crusted backs.

The secret of the Curse was here — the beetles had dwelt within the body of the mummy! They had eaten it out and nested within, and at night they crawled forth. It was true then!

I screamed once when the thought hit me, and dashed back to Hartley's bedroom. I could hear the sound of footsteps ascending the outer stairs; the police were on their way, but I couldn't wait. I raced into the bedroom, dread tugging at my heart.

Had Hartley's story been true, after all? Were the beetles really messengers of a divine vengeance?

I ran into that bedroom where Arthur Hartley lay, stooped over his huddled figure on the bed. My hands fumbled over his body, searching for a wound. I had to know how he had died.

But there was no blood, there was no mark, and there was no weapon beside him. It had been shock or heart attack, after all. I was strangely relieved when I thought of this. I stood up and eased the body back again on the pillows.

I felt almost glad, because during my search my hands had moved over the body while my eyes roved over the room. I was looking for beetles.

Hartley had feared the beetles — the beetles that crawled out of the mummy. They had crawled every night, if his story was to be believed; crawled into his room, up the bed-posts, across the pillows.

Where were they now? They had left the mummy and disappeared, and Hartley was dead. Where were they?

Suddenly I stared again at Hartley. There was something wrong with the body on the bed. When I had lifted the corpse it seemed singularly light for a man of Hartley's build. As I gazed at him now, he seemed empty of more than life. I peered into that ravaged face more closely, and then I shuddered. For the cords on his neck moved convulsively, his chest seemed to rise and fall, his head fell sideways on the pillow. He lived — or something inside him did!

And then as his twisted features moved, I cried aloud, for I knew how Hartley had died, and what had killed him; knew the secret of the Scarab Curse and why the beetles crawled out of the mummy to seek his bed. I knew what they had meant to do — what, tonight, they had done. I cried aloud as I saw Hartley's face move, in hopes that my voice would drown that dreadful rustling sound which filled the room and came from *inside Hartley's body.*

I knew that the Scarab Curse had killed him, and I screamed quite wildly as his mouth gaped slowly open. Just as I fainted, I saw Arthur Hartley's dead lips part, allowing a rustling swarm of *black Scarabæus beetles* to pour out across the pillow.

Ω

# BEETLES TELEPLAY

## by Robert Bloch

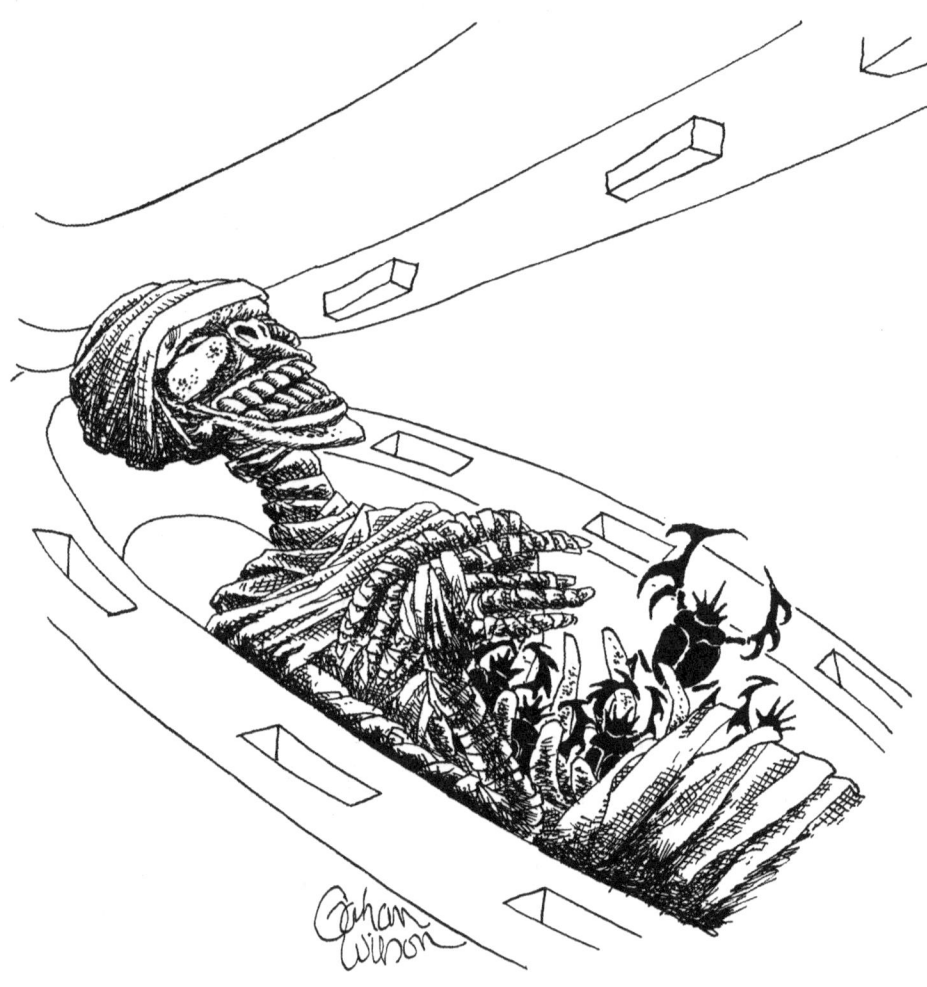

BEETLES

Teleplay by Robert Bloch

Based on a short story
by Robert Bloch

©1986 Laurel-T.V. Inc.

---

## Prelude

SCENE 1
FADE IN:

INT. COTTAGE -- PARLOR -- DAY                    [Interior]

Against a bright wall BG [BackGround], the CU [CloseUp]
SHADOW of a HUGE CROCODILE'S HEAD moves across screen.
CAMERA PULLS BACK and we see the stuffed body, mounted on a
stand, carried through OPEN front doorway INTO the room by
two English moving men, SID and BERT.

Gingerly, they set it down against a side-wall amidst a
clutter of tall crates and bulky packing-cases. Sid is so
eager to let go that he almost tips it over, and Bert gives
him a reproving frown.

>                    BERT
> Easy, now! It won't bite.

>                    SID
> Don't be too sure.
>                         (shakes head)
> Look at those teeth -- like a bloody buzz-saw.

Sid breaks off, following Bert's glance toward the doorway
as ARTHUR HARTLEY, a scholarly-looking type in his late
thirties, ENTERS from doorway, WHEELING a crate shaped like
a coffin. Bert moves to him.

>                    BERT
> 'Ere -- let me give you a hand.

>                    HARTLEY
>                         (shakes head)
> Don't touch it!
>                         (forces smile)
> I can manage. This is the last one.

Hartley eases the crate off the handcart and leans it
against the wall.

>                    BERT
> Want us to open these crates for you,
> Guv'nor?

>                    HARTLEY
> No, I'll handle them.

> SID
> Sure you don't need help?

> HARTLEY
> Never mind.

Sid glances at the upright crate against the wall.

> SID
> What about this 'ere coffin?

> HARTLEY
> (overreacting)
> Coffin? Who told you that?

> SID
> (apologetic)
> Sorry, guv'nor -- I was only thinking --

> HARTLEY
> Never mind!

Hartley moves to front door -- YANKS it OPEN -- then turns to confront Sid and Bert.

> HARTLEY (continued)
> Just clear out now -- both of you! I know
> what I'm doing!

Sid and Bert exchange glances, puzzled by this sudden outburst. Then they move to doorway and EXIT. Hartley peers after them thru doorway.

> HARTLEY (continued)
> It's not a coffin. Remember that -- it's not
> a coffin!

Hartley SLAMS door SHUT.

---

SCENE 2

INT. COTTAGE -- PARLOR -- DUSK

Lamps are LIT around the room and in their play of light and shadow we see open crates and boxes piled against wall near front door. Now the other walls are lined with statues of Egyptian animal-headed gods. CAMERA PANS ACROSS THEM and OVER glass cases holding jars -- then HOLDS on coffin-shaped crate, still unopened, standing alone in corner.

Hartley, at table in center of room, OPENS drawer and TAKES OUT a chisel. Moving to crate, he gently inserts chisel to pry it open. The lid LOOSENS and Hartley REMOVES it to reveal -- in CU -- an ornate, gilded upright mummy-case with a female face.

Hartley stares at it gloating; we sense his eagerness to open it as he lifts chisel again -- then FREEZES at SOUND OF KNOCKING at front door.

---

SCENE 3

Hartley, disturbed, listens as KNOCK SOUNDS AGAIN -- LOUDER

and more INSISTENT TEMPO. Frowning, Hartley moves to door, halting before it. A MUFFLED VOICE CALLS from outside.

> HAMID BEY (o.c. [off camera])
> Mr. Hartley? Arthur Hartley?

> HARTLEY
> Yes. What is it?

> HAMID BEY (o.c.)
> I must talk to you.

> HARTLEY
> Sorry -- I'm very busy. Come back tomorrow.

> HAMID BEY (o.c.)
> Tomorrow may be too late. I must see you -- now.

Hartley hesitates, glancing over at the mummy-case. Then, making a reluctant decision, he OPENS the door. CAMERA MOVES IN on HAMID BEY -- a hawkfaced old Egyptian wearing a caftan. He nods at Hartley, stepping across threshold.

> HAMID BEY
> May I come in?

Hartley, taken by surprise, can't prevent his entry. He stares, puzzled, as Hamid Bey CLOSES door.

> HARTLEY
> What are you doing?

> HAMID BEY
> It is best we speak privately.

> HARTLEY
> Who are you?

> HAMID BEY
> My name is Hamid Bey.

Hamid Bey moves past Hartley, then halts at center of the room, glancing at the statuary lining the walls. He nods.

> HAMID BEY
> Very impressive. You have a remarkable collection, Mr. Hartley.

> HARTLEY
> How did you know my name?

> HAMID BEY
> I know a great deal about you, Mr. Hartley. You're an American -- an amateur archaeologist -- and a thief.

> HARTLEY
> Now see here --

> HAMID BEY
> (calmly)
> Every one of these pieces was stolen. Smuggled out of that secret tomb you discovered in the desert below Karnak.

                        HARTLEY
                    (on the alert)
Who sent you -- the government? Or was it
Interpol?

                        HAMID BEY
Nobody sent me. I came here to warn you.

---

SCENE 4

    Hamid Bey moves to the mummy-case. Hartley intercepts him.

                        HARTLEY
Don't touch that!

                        HAMID BEY
I have no intention of doing so.

Hamid Bey gestures toward a metal band on the edge of the
case near the gilded face. It ears a raised scarab figure
with lines of ideographs beside it.

                        HAMID BEY (continued)
This is the seal of Kephra -- the beetle-god
of ancient Egypt. Do you know what that
means?

                        HARTLEY
That's why I'm here -- to do research on my
findings at the British Museum. I can't read
these inscriptions.

                        HAMID BEY
Then allow me. This case contains the body of
a temple virgin who violated her vows. She
was put to death and cursed. And anyone who
disturbs her mummy will share that curse. I
came only to claim the case and return it to
its rightful resting-place.

                        HARTLEY
                    (flaring up)
Do you think I'm a fool? Mummies like this
were buried with their personal jewelry.
That's what you're really after, isn't it? A
fortune in precious stones --

                        HAMID BEY
Please, Mr. Hartley. I'm warning you --

                        HARTLEY
                    (fists clenched)
And I'm warning you. Get out and stay out!

                        HAMID BEY
                    (shrugs)
As you wish.

    Hamid Bey moves to front door -- OPENS it -- turns.

                        HAMID BEY (continued)
I am staying in the village, at the inn. If

you change your mind you can reach me there.

                    HARTLEY
                 (steps forward)
     Out!

Hamid Bey EXITS. Hartley crosses to door, CLOSES and LOCKS
it. Turning, he moves to the mummy-case.

---

SCENE 5

     As he stoops to pick up the chisel lying on the floor beside
     it, his scowl is transformed to an eager smile. He carefully
     PRIES OFF the metal band with its scarab figure POCKETS IT.
     Then he raises the chisel again to edge of mummy-case near
     its face.

                    HARTLEY (continued)
                      (murmurs)
     Now --
                                             CUT TO:

---

SCENE 6

     INT. COTTAGE -- PARLOR -- DUSK

     ANOTHER ANGLE ON HARTLEY at mummy-case. The lid is now off,
     standing beside the OPEN case, which reveals an upright
     mummy. Hartley is UNWINDING wrappings covering its face. As
     it appears, he halts, staring. CAMERA IN to HOLD on mummy's
     shrivelled features and we see that its eye-sockets contain
     two huge rubies.

                    HARTLEY
                      (exultant)
     I was right!

     CAMERA PULLS BACK. Hartley takes a pouch from his jacket-
     pocket, OPENS it. Then, with his free hand, he carefully
     PLUCKS the rubies from the mummy's eye-sockets. Cupping the
     jewels, he stares at them.

                    HARTLEY (continued)
     Magnificent! Absolutely magnificent!
                      (smiling, he nods at mummy)
     Thanks, old girl!

     DROPPING rubies into pouch, he carries it across room to
     inner doorway at opposite side. CAMERA MOVES IN to HOLD in
     CU on MUMMY'S FACE -- empty eye-sockets sightlessly staring
     and open mouth fixed in a ghastly grin.

---

SCENE 7

     INT. COTTAGE -- BEDROOM -- NIGHT

     MATCHING CU of HARTLEY'S FACE on pillow, eyes closed in
     sleep. CAMERA PULLS OUT and we see him lying in bed, the
     pouch resting on pillow behind his head. The only light-
     source is MOON-RAYS from the open window beyond the bed at
     far wall. And now this becomes the source of sound -- as

EERY PIPING begins to ECHO FAINTLY from somewhere outside.

CLOSER ON HARTLEY as PIPING RISES. He stirs, opens his eyes. Startled, he raises himself on one elbow, gazing toward window. Then, quickly, he turns to glance down at the pouch on the pillow -- and he GASPS in shock, drawing his hand back.

CU of POUCH. Resting atop it is a HUGE BLACK BEETLE. The OS [OffStage] PIPING RISES TO A SCREECHING CRESCENDO.

CLOSE ON HARTLEY. He stares, horrified -- turns away to CLAW AT the light-switch on lamp atop bedside table between bed and window. The LAMPLIGHT TURNS ON. As it does so, the OS PIPING HALTS ABRUPTLY.

Hartley turns back and glances down. CAMERA MOVES IN ON POUCH on pillow. The beetle has disappeared.

Smiling in rueful relief, Hartley shakes his head, murmuring to himself.

>                    HARTLEY
>      Nightmare. Only a nightmare --

Clutching pouch in one hand, he settles back down on pillow, as CAMERA MOVES IN on him for CU. Suddenly his expression changes and we see the doubt in his eyes.

>                    HARTLEY (continued)
>      Or was it --?

>           End of Prelude

---

>           ACT I

SCENE 8

FADE IN

>      INT. COTTAGE -- PARLOR -- DAY

Hartley ENTERS through doorway, carrying a coffee-pot. He crosses to table. A chair has been drawn up beside it and on its surface we see the pouch containing the jewels, a note-pad, and a cup and saucer. He moves up beside the table, ready to pour coffee into the cup. As he does so he glances down -- and FREEZES.

---

Beetle A

CU of CUP, from HIGH ANGLE -- so that we can see what he sees. Inside the cup, against its white base, is the moving form of a BLACK BEETLE.

---

CU of Hartley's shocked stare. CAMERA PULLS OUT as Hartley SLAMS the coffee-pot down on the table-top. Grabbing the cup, he HURLS it to the floor. It SHATTERS. Hartley looks down and CAMERA PANS with his gaze, then HOLDS on broken fragments of cup on the floor below. All we see are the broken pieces -- the beetle is gone.

ANGLE ON HARTLEY as he frowns, bewildered -- his eyes darting to scan the floor in search of the beetle. It's nowhere in sight. He blinks, rubs his eyes.

PHONE RINGS OS and Hartley crosses to an end-table near the doorway and lifts the receiver, speaking into the mouthpiece.

                    HARTLEY
          Hello --

                    HAMID BEY'S VOICE
                      (from phone)
          Good morning, Mr. Hartley.

                    HARTLEY
                      (disconcerted)
          Hamid Bey?

                    HAMID BEY'S VOICE
                      (from phone)
          I trust you had a good night's rest. Or did
          you?

                    HARTLEY
          What do you want?

                    HAMID BEY'S VOICE
                      (from phone)
          The mummy. Are you ready to give it to me
          now?

                    HARTLEY
                      (angrily)
          Go to hell!

He SLAMS receiver down. Turning, he shakes his head, muttering to himself.

                    HARTLEY (continued)
          A trick -- that's what it is! Some kind of a
          trick.
                                        CUT TO:

---

SCENE 9

          INT. COTTAGE -- BATHROOM -- DAY

          Hartley moves to washstand with wall-mirror above it. He takes a cordless shaver from open case on counter and raises it, preparing to shave. Then he hesitates as he hears FAINT SOUND OF PIPING OS

          Hartley turns, frowning. Shaver in hand, he moves to the open bathroom window and peers out. As he does so, piping stops abruptly. Hartley glances out again, but it's apparent from his puzzled face that he sees nothing.

          Moving back to washstand, he FLICKS shaver ON. Simultaneously with BUZZ OF SHAVER we hear OS PIPING BEGIN AGAIN. Hartley doesn't notice it. He raises shaver to his

face -- confronts himself in the mirror -- then lowers
shaver as he stares at --

---

CU (SFX [Special Effects]) OF MIRROR -- HARTLEY'S POV [Point
of View]

Beetles B

His IMAGE FADES, DISSOLVING in a SWIRL OF MIST. As OS PIPING
RISES we see a ROUND BLACK SHAPE FORM in the SWIRL -- then
it ENLARGES -- and we recognize the hideous visage of a
BLACK BEETLE -- EXPANDING as it ZOOMS FORWARD to FILL THE
MIRROR with its ferocious face.

Hartley, horrified, DROPS shaver on counter -- turns -- and
rushes to EXIT thru bathroom doorway.

---

INT. ANGLE ON COTTAGE DOOR -- DAY

As it is FLUNG OPEN and Hartley EMERGES, glancing forwards
at SOUND OF PIPING OS. But now, as he steps out, the PIPING
HALTS. Hartley peers OS again.

---

SCENE 10

CAMERA PANS WITH HIS GAZE to reveal the empty lawn -- a
cluster of trees and shrubbery bordering one side,
shimmering in peaceful sunlight.

CAMERA TO HARTLEY. He shrugs, relieved -- muttering.

> HARTLEY
> Nerves --

He turns away in doorway and we

CUT TO:

---

SCENE 11

INT. COTTAGE -- BATHROOM -- DAY

Hartley ENTERS thru doorway, then halts, obviously unwilling
to face the bathroom mirror. Squaring his shoulders, he
forces himself to lift his gaze.

CAMERA IN to HOLD ON MIRROR. The glass is clear.

CLOSE ON HARTLEY -- nodding, grimfaced.

> HARTLEY
> Nerves!

CUT TO:

---

SCENE 12

INT. COTTAGE -- PARLOR -- DAY

Hartley sits before table, center. Atop it, the pouch and a
magnifying glass. He OPENS pouch and takes out a ruby --
picks up magnifying glass and stares at the gem -- then
smiles.

HARTLEY

Priceless --

Still holding glass and examining gem on table-top, he
reaches into the pouch with his free hand to bring out the
other ruby. But when he withdraws his hand from the pouch
there is something in his curled palm which causes his
smile to vanish. Quickly his hand opens -- and what FALLS
from it to the table-top is --

---

Beetle C

ZOOM to CU of BEETLE on table. It is twitching -- wriggling
its feelers and mandibles; a gruesome black monstrosity.

---

CU of Hartley's shocked reaction.

CAMERA PULLS OUT as he raises his fist. CAMERA FOLLOWS FIST
as it SMASHES DOWN on the beetle.

Hartley stares down at beetle BELOW FRAME. He's dazed. PHONE
RINGS OS and jars him into a blinking awareness.

---

SCENE 13

As PHONE RINGS AGAIN he pushes chair back, RISES, and
crosses to end-table to pick up receiver. He hears

HAMID BEY'S VOICE
(from phone)

Mr. Hartley?

HARTLEY

You again --

HAMID BEY'S VOICE
(from phone)
This is your final warning. I will come to
you at dusk.

There is a CLICK and a BUZZING SOUND as the line goes dead.
Hartley, stunned, drops the receiver into its cradle.
Slowly, he glances up toward the window.

CAMERA TO WINDOW -- HOLDING on sunlight beyond the window-
frame.

DISSOLVE TO:

---

SCENE 14

INT. -- COTTAGE -- PARLOR -- DUSK

MATCHING CU of WINDOW-FRAME -- but now there is no sunlight;
DARKNESS is gathering beyond. We hear a HISSING SOUND OS

CAMERA PULLS OUT and we see Hartley, moving around the
parlor -- holding a spray-can of insecticide. This is the
source of the HISSING as he SPRAYS the fumes around the edge
of the flooring at the base of the walls, grimly intent on
his task. Lamps have been LIT and behind the statues of the
Egyptian gods their grotesque shadows loom. Hartley moves

past them, SPRAYING their animal-heads. He approaches the open mummy-case and raises the spray-can -- but before he can press the nozzle, a KNOCK SOUNDS at the front door.

Hartley's scowl tells us he knows who's outside. He glances toward the door, calling.

> HARTLEY
> Go away!

He is answered by ANOTHER KNOCKING SOUND.

> HARTLEY (continued)
> Go away, I tell you!

KNOCKING RESUMES -- LOUDER, INSISTENT. Hartley shakes his head angrily. But the KNOCKING IS STACCATO now. Hartley takes a deep breath. Then he STRIDES to front door and OPENS it with his free hand -- the other still holding the spray-can.

---

SCENE 15

Hamid Bey stands before the open doorway, his face impassive as he bows slightly.

> HAMID BEY
> I am sorry to disturb you, Mr. Hartley.

Hartley's forced smile is mocking; his voice has a sarcastic edge.

> HARTLEY
> Disturb me? There's nothing to be disturbed about.
>> (steps aside)
> Here -- see for yourself.

---

SCENE 16

Hamid Bey ENTERS. Hartley CLOSES door, eyeing his visitor as Hamid Bey glances around room. His gaze fixes on the open mummy-case.

> HAMID BEY
> I see you chose to disregard my warning.

Hartley follows his glance and nods.

> HARTLEY
> About the mummy-case? Yes, I opened it.

> HAMID BEY
> What happened then?

> HARTLEY
> Nothing.

> HAMID BEY
> Nothing?

> HARTLEY
> Did you think the mummy would come to life?
>> (shakes head)
> That thing in the case died three thousand

years ago. It can't harm me.

                    HAMID BEY
The mummy is dead. But the curse is still
alive. The curse of Kephra -- the Beetle God
of Egypt.

                    HARTLEY
You're talking nonsense!

Hamid Bey eyes the spray-can Hartley is holding.

                    HAMID BEY
I see you've done some spraying.

                    HARTLEY
This cottage has been vacant all year. I just
got rid of a few insects.

                    HAMID BEY
What sort of insects, Mr. Hartley?

                    HARTLEY
It doesn't matter.
                         (puts can on table)
They're gone now.

                    HAMID BEY
But they will return.

                    HARTLEY
How do you know?
                    HAMID BEY
The gods of ancient Egypt have not vanished.
And we who are faithful remain to serve them.

                    HARTLEY
That's just superstition.

                    HAMID BEY
Is it? I myself am a priest of the Old
Religion. And I tell you the power of the
gods is real. That is why you must give the
mummy back to me.
                         (eyes pouch)
The mummy -- and the jewels.

---

SCENE 17
                    HARTLEY
So that's it!

Hartley moves to the table, blocking Hamid Bey from a view
of the pouch -- and cupping the ruby beside it in his hand.

                    HARTLEY (continued)
You were after the rubies all along, weren't
you? Playing tricks to scare me! Well, it
didn't work --

Hamid Bey gestures.

                    HAMID BEY
Please, Mr. Hartley -- you're making a

**41**

mistake. No one can defy the gods. For the
sake of your life, I beg you --

He takes a step toward Hartley. As he does so, Hartley's
hand DIPS into his jacket pocket and EMERGES holding a
revolver levelled at Hamid Bey.

> HARTLEY
> For the sake of your life -- get out!

There's a CLICK as Hartley THUMBS the safety-catch. He steps
forward, and Hamid Bey retreats -- backing to front door.
Hartley advances, training his weapon on Hamid Bey.

> HAMID BEY
> No -- remember the curse! This is your last
> chance --

Hartley steps past him, then FLINGS the door OPEN with his
free hand. Turning, he aims at Hamid Bey

> HARTLEY
> (grimly)
> And this is yours. Now -- go!

Hamid Bey SIGHS and shrugs in surrender.

> HAMID BEY
> If you insist. But one last word, Mr.
> Hartley. Whatever you do -- if you value your
> life -- don't touch that mummy!

Turning, Hamid Bey EXITS. Hartley SLAMS door SHUT after him,
LOCKS it. Turning, he slumps against it, breathing heavily,
his eyes closed in relief.

---

SCENE 18

> HARTLEY
> (murmurs)
> Crazy! The man's a lunatic. Don't touch the
> mummy, he says --

> HARTLEY (continued)
> Don't touch that mummy --
> (nods, smiles)
> So that's it!

Pocketing the revolver, he moves forward. CAMERA GOES WITH
HIM and HOLDS as he halts before the open upright mummy-
case, nodding at its fleshless features.

> HARTLEY (continued)
> I should have guessed. Those jewels in the
> eyes aren't the only ones.

Hartley reaches out and grasps the end of the mummy-
wrappings which dangles at its withered neck. He starts to
pull it aside, grinning at the grisly face.

> HARTLEY (continued)
> All right, old girl -- let's see what else
> you're hiding!

Hartley tugs at the wrappings. Dust rises, but the wrappings are congealed and don't budge. Hartley tugs harder -- the wrappings hold. He scowls.

>                    HARTLEY (continued)
>          Damn!

He releases his grip on the mummy. Reaching into his trouser-pocket he pulls out a switchblade knife, FLICKS catch -- and the blade SPRINGS UP.

>                    HARTLEY (continued)
>          Sorry -- but if that's the way you want it --

He JABS the blade forward, SLASHING at the wrappings, then pulls them away from the mummy's body to reveal outline of wrapped arms folded upwards against the chest. He RIPS at the cloth covering the joined hands -- TEARS it aside -- stares in surprise.

CU of MUMMY -- its wrappings ripped and dangling from hands clasped together on its chest. They clutch an oblong case bearing a beetle design.

Hartley, excited, PULLS case free. He OPENS lid and stares down, eyes elated.

CU -- OPEN CASE -- its contents a glittering mass of chains, bracelets and rings studded with gems.

>                    HARTLEY'S VOICE
>          I was right!
>                              CUT TO:

---

SCENE 19

    INT. COTTAGE -- PARLOR -- NIGHT

    Hartley, seated at table, DUMPS jewelry from case. He picks up a bracelet and admires it, nodding.

>                    HARTLEY
>          Flawless. This stuff must be worth a fortune!

    FAINT SOUND OF PIPING OS. Hartley puts bracelet down and glances toward front door with a frown.

>                    HARTLEY (continued)
>          More tricks?
>                         (rises)
>          We'll see about that.

---

SCENE 19A

    CAMERA WITH HARTLEY as he strides to front door -- UNLOCKS and OPENS it. PIPING LOUDER OS. He peers thru doorway, PULLING revolver from his pocket.

>                    HARTLEY (continued)
>                         (calls)
>          I know you're out there! Stop that damned
>          noise and go away!

The OS PIPING RISES. So does Hartley's anger.

                    HARTLEY (continued)
     I warned you!

He levels revolver and EXITS thru doorway.

A SUCCESSION OF CUs QUICK GLIMPSES of ANIMAL HEADS OF
STATUES lining wall -- PUNCTUATED by SOUND OF REVOLVER SHOTS
OS in RAPID SUCCESSION. At SOUND OF SIXTH SHOT the PIPING
HALTS.

ANGLE ON OPEN FRONT DOORWAY as HARTLEY ENTERS. He pockets
revolver, BREATHING HEAVILY, then glances up at statue of
Anubis, smiling.

                    HARTLEY (continued)
     Nobody there. Scared him off!

---

SCENE 19

     Hartley turns, CLOSES and LOCKS door, then moves to a wall-
     cabinet standing beside Anubis. He smiles, addressing the
     jackal-headed figure.

                    HARTLEY (continued)
     All clear now. No more tricks.

     Hartley OPENS cabinet -- PULLS OUT a bottle of whiskey --
     then a glass.

                    HARTLEY (continued)
     Calls for a celebration, don't you think?

     CAMERA WITH HARTLEY as he turns, crossing to table,
     grinning. Placing glass and bottle on table-top, he glances
     down -- and his grin dissolves into a look of panic.

     CLOSE HIGH ANGLE on TABLE-TOP. We see the bottle, the glass,
     the open jewel-case with lid beside it as before. But the
     heap of jewelry is gone.

                    HARTLEY'S VOICE
     The jewels!
                         (despairingly)
     What happened to my jewels?

                    End of Act I

---

                    Act II

SCENE 20

     INT. COTTAGE -- PARLOR -- NIGHT

     Hartley stands at table, eyes frantic as he scans the bare
     surface where the jewelry had rested.

                    HARTLEY
     Where are they? How could they disappear?

     Turning, he glances at floor under and beside table. Nothing
     there. He moves away, eyeing the floor anxiously. CAMERA

GOES WITH HIM as he confronts the row of animal-headed
statues. Hysteria grips him.

> HARTLEY (continued)
> Am I crazy? I saw them -- you saw them! What
> became of my jewels? Tell me!

The animal-heads leer silently. Hartley gets control of
himself, shaking his head self-consciously.

> HARTLEY (continued)
> Sorry. You can't tell me anything, can you?
> You're just a bunch of silly statues.
> > (nods)
> And I'm a fool. This is another one of Hamid
> Bey's tricks. But how could he do it?
> > (scowling)
> Think! There's got to be an answer -- got to
> be.
> > (shrugs)
> Why am I talking to myself? What I need right
> now is a drink.

Hartley turns, CAMERA MOVING WITH HIM to table. He starts to
reach for bottle -- halts -- stares down, his eyes widening.

> HARTLEY (continued)
> Well I'll be damned!

CU -- TABLE-TOP. We see bottle, glass, jewel-case, lid. And
heaped beside them, the jewelry as before.

ANGLE ON HARTLEY. He grins, surprised and delighted.

> HARTLEY (continued)
> Must have been here all the time! Had to be.
> > (nods)
> Hypnosis. Sure, that's what it was. That old
> devil -- he hypnotized me!

Hartley THUMPS glass onto table-top, UNCORKS the bottle, and
POURS glass FULL. Smiling at his solution of the mystery, he
raises the glass, glancing toward the animal-headed statues
along the side wall.

> HARTLEY (continued)
> A toast, gentlemen. Here's to the gods of
> Egypt -- because you're dead! You're dead --
> and I'm alive!

He DOWNS the drink at a gulp. Setting the glass on the
table, Hartley turns to nod at the open mummy-case on the
wall behind him, and the upright mummy standing within it.

> HARTLEY (continued)
> You hear me, old girl? I'm alive!

CHUCKLING happily, Hartley crosses to the mummy-case,
carrying the open bottle. He halts before it, blinking at
the shrivelled face with its empty eye-sockets -- then holds
out the bottle in mock invitation.

> HARTLEY (continued)
> How about it? You want to drink to that?

The mummy's silent stare changes Hartley's mood. He pulls
bottle back, frowning, and shakes his head.

> HARTLEY (continued)
> Party-pooper! Who needs you?

He raises bottle, DRINKS from it -- then lowers bottle
again, scowling at the mummy.

> HARTLEY (continued)
> Temple virgin, eh? You and your curses -- and
> your ugly face! Stop staring at me!

Reaching out, he CLOSES the lid of the mummy-case.

> HARTLEY (continued)
> There -- you can stay in that case until you
> rot. I'm not afraid of you any more! Or Hamid
> Bey!

Turning, he moves to table. CAMERA IN as he seats himself,
raising the bottle, his grin defiant.

> HARTLEY (continued)
> Not afraid of anyone!

Tilting the bottle up, Hartley DRINKS.

                                                    CUT TO

---

SCENE 21

    INT. COTTAGE -- PARLOR -- NIGHT

    CU -- WHISKY BOTTLE on table. It's nearly empty.

    CAMERA TO HARTLEY. He's obviously nearly full. Slumped back
    in his chair, eyes closed, we hear his WHEEZY GASPING
    BREATHING. And now -- from OS -- the SOUND OF EERY PIPING
    RISES.

                                                    CUT TO

---

SCENE 10 CONT.

    EXT. LAWN BEFORE COTTAGE -- NIGHT

    PIPING GROWS LOUDER as CAMERA PANS ACROSS LAWN to a cluster
    of dark shrubbery and trees bordering one side. CAMERA MOVES
    THRU TREES to HOLD ON HAMID BEY. He stands there playing his
    WEIRD MELODY on a flute.

                                                    CUT TO

---

SCENE 21 CONT.

    INT. COTTAGE -- PARLOR -- NIGHT

    Hartley in chair as before, SNORING, sound asleep. OS PIPING
    SHRILLS HIGHER but he doesn't stir.

    CAMERA PANS AWAY -- ACROSS stone statues against the wall;
    animal-heads poised as though listening. Now CAMERA MOVES TO
    HOLD on CLOSED MUMMY-CASE on far wall behind Hartley. As
    PIPING SQUEALS OS, the lid of the mummy-case SWINGS OPEN

slowly to reveal the mummy.

---

CAMERA ON BASE of case. Now, from behind the mummy's feet, a SWARM OF BLACK BEETLES starts to crawl forth -- first a TRICKLE -- then a MOVING MASS.

Beetles D.

CAMERA GOES WITH BEETLES as they CRAWL OUT across the floor -- moving to the chair where Hartley sprawls in stupor. OS PIPING RISES TO A SCREECH.

CLOSE ON HARTLEY -- as he STIRS -- BLINKS -- then glances down in horror.

QUICK-CUT CUs -- Beetles on Hartley's shoes and ankles -- Beetles CRAWLING up his legs -- then his waist, etc.

ANGLE ON HARTLEY -- as he SCREAMS -- flails out to brush beetles off -- tries to rise -- then FALLS BACK unconscious in his chair as the twitching, clawing black beetles swarm up over his motionless form while OS PIPING SHRILLS TO CRESCENDO.

CUT TO

---

SCENE 22

EXT. LAWN BEFORE COTTAGE -- DAY

RICHARDS, a well-dressed London ``City'' type, wearing a bowler, moves up the walk. He glances up as he hears

                      CONSTABLE'S VOICE
Detective Richards?

                      CONSTABLE
Constable Higbsby, sir.

                      RICHARDS
Right.
                (gestures towards door)
Have you spoken to Mr. Hartley yet?

                      CONSTABLE
I was waiting for you, like I said I would.

                      RICHARDS
You said a lot of things, Constable, that don't really add up. Statues, jewels, and a curse involving bloody beetles.

                      CONSTABLE
Well this Hamid Bey . . .

                      RICHARDS
Ah yes, where IS this mysterious Egyptian?

                      CONSTABLE
                (slightly embarrassed)
Uh, I'm afraid he left the inn shortly after he rang me this morning. Maybe Mr. Hartley knows where he went.

**47**

>                    RICHARDS
>                 (growing impatient)
>      What do you say we find out?

Constable nods and knocks on the door. There is no answer.
He knocks again. Same result.

>                    CONSTABLE
>      Seems he's not in.

Richards moves past him to grasp the door knob.

>                    RICHARDS
>      Suppose we try this.

Richards turns the knob and the door opens. The Constable
gapes, surprised.

>                    CONSTABLE
>      But, sir --

>                    RICHARDS
>      I didn't make this trip just to listen to
>      tall tales.

---

SCENE 23

INT. COTTAGE -- PARLOR -- DAY

As Richards and Constable MOVE IN from doorway -- then HALT
-- glancing in surprise at the statues leering from the
walls in lamplight -- the open mummy-case on the side-wall.
The Constable nods excitedly.

>                    CONSTABLE
>      You see, sir? Statues -- just like he said!

Richards glances OS (forward) and his eyes narrow.

>                    RICHARDS
>      Never mind the statues.

CAMERA PANS WITH HIS GAZE to Hartley, seated at table in
center of room, his BACK TO CAMERA.

WIDE ANGLE INC. Richards and Constable. They exchange
puzzled glances. Then the Constable calls out.

>                    CONSTABLE
>      Mr. Hartley?

CLOSE ON HARTLEY -- BACK TO CAMERA. Motionless, he doesn't
respond.

>                    CONSTABLE'S VOICE
>      Mr. Hartley --

CAMERA TO Richards and Constable. Their glances are troubled
now. CAMERA WITH THEM as they cross to table behind Hartley
-- peer around the back of his chair.

CU -- HARTLEY. His head rests against the chair-back -- eyes
wide with horror, face frozen in fear.

WIDER ANGLE INC. RICHARDS, CONSTABLE. The Constable looks

shocked. Richards frowns.

                    RICHARDS
        The man's dead.

CAMERA PANS WITH HIS GLANCE TO TABLE-TOP. We see the whisky-
bottle -- jewel-case and lid -- and the glittering pile of
jewelry.

                    CONSTABLE'S VOICE
        Look -- the jewels!

ANGLE ON RICHARDS, CONSTABLE, HARTLEY

                    RICHARDS
                    (nods)
        At least we know it wasn't a robbery.

                    CONSTABLE
                    (puzzled)
        I don't understand. Look -- there's no
        beetles here. What killed him?

Richards reaches down to touch Hartley's shoulder.

---

SCENE 24

        Hartley's body sways -- his head drops back further -- and
        his jaws OPEN.

        CU -- CONSTABLE AND RICHARDS -- as they GASP.

BEETLES E.

        CU -- HARTLEY'S FACE. From his gaping mouth there CRAWLS a
        SWARM OF BLACK BEETLES.

                    THE END

# ROBERT BLOCH: WRITER & GENTLEMAN

## by Hugh B. Cave

Robert Bloch and I have been around awhile. We both wrote for many of the old pulp-paper magazines, including the original *Weird Tales*. When the pulps died, Bob soared off into radio, novels, movie and TV scripts while I moved into books and the slicks. Surprisingly, we didn't come face to face until we were co-guests of honor at the 1983 Pulpcon in Dayton, Ohio.

It was an odd sort of meeting. By the best of good luck we arrived at the Dayton airport within moments of each other, and my airline had lost part of my return ticket. While they looked for it, Bob and I sat on a bench for forty-five minutes and reminisced about old times. By the time we reached the Dayton University convention scene we were old friends.

But I had been reading Bob's books and stories, hearing his radio dramas and watching his work on TV and in the movies for years and years. And I had admired just about everything this man did.

There isn't space here to go through Robert Bloch's long, long list of works and discuss individual achievements. Anyway, the man should be taken as a whole, first for his wit and warmth, then for the impact he has had on the field of the macabre in general. More than any other writer, it was Bloch who ventured — perhaps I should say *adventured* — away from the old weird-fiction themes and began finding new kinds of horror in the minds of ordinary people in ordinary places.

If you line up a collection of today's horror novels and read a couple of chapters in each, you'll discover something else to admire about Mr. Bloch. He is one of the very few fantasy writers left who use the English language the way it was meant to be used — as a tool of communication. While newer writers ruthlessly monkey around with it, often using it as a means of *hiding* from the reader what they are talking about — because, I suppose, they think such deception makes them look "clever" or "deep" — Bloch *wants* the reader to understand what he is saying, and makes certain the reader does so. You don't find Mr. B. indulging in the kind of deliberate obscurity that leaves a reader, at the end of a story, angry with himself for "not getting" what the tale is about. Bob turns out a prose that is easy to read and seems so deceptively easy to write, but that actually demands not only consummate skill but a conscience and a caring.

At a convention panel on which Bob and I both appeared, someone asked the question, "If you could choose any one writer with whom you would like to collaborate on a novel, who would it be?" I had only to point to Robert Bloch and say, "That bloke, because working with him would be a learning experience." It would be, too. Not to mention a heap of fun.                                        Ω

*Hugh B. Cave is the author of some 800 pulp-magazine stories, 350 slick-magazine stories, and 30 books, several of which have been bookclub selections. His most recent novel is* Disciples of Dread *(Tor). Coming soon from the same publisher is* The Lower Deep.

# WEIRD TALES TALKS WITH ROBERT BLOCH

## by Bob Morrish

**Weird Tales:** You've been writing for over 50 years now. During that time, you've had a prime vantage point from which to view the development of horror and speculative fiction — its overall appeal, its readers, its markets. Based upon interaction with editors, fan letters, feedback at conventions, and so on, what kind of discernible changes have you seen over the years?

**Bloch:** Most of the fears remain the same after a half-century or more — people today are still afraid of the dark, startled by a loud, unexpected noise, don't feel comfortable spending the night alone in a graveyard, morgue, or even a wax museum. There's still an aversion to haunted houses, an antipathy towards snakes, rats, spiders, and unmuzzled coloratura sopranos. Fears of pain, suffering, and death never seem to alter — though today such fears may be directed to different *sources*.

**WT:** Have you observed correlations between larger issues — the world at war, the state of the national economy, etc. — and the tone of popular fiction?

**Bloch:** I detect a greater cynicism now than in the past. What was once regarded as "immorality" has become "human nature," and characters formerly labeled "anti-heroes" are today accepted as the heroic norm.

**WT:** Have you ever consciously tailored your work to fit the prevailing mood of the times?

**Bloch:** I have consciously tailored what I write to my *own* "prevailing mood" of the moment. Becoming cynical at the age of five probably helped give me a head start.

**WT:** Do you sense any particular "fears" which have emerged (or re-emerged) in society as a whole of late (not in a very specific sense — as in "fear of AIDS" — but rather in a more generic sense)?

**Bloch:** The particular fear which seems to have emerged (or re-emerged) in society of late is the fear of others. In the time since I began writing professionally, there have been profound changes in social attitudes. People in urban and many suburban areas no longer leave their doors unlocked, don't allow strangers into the house without identification, take precautions to protect their homes, cars, and wallets. And in the larger cities, there are ever-enlarging portions of the business and residential neighborhoods where ordinary citizens are afraid to walk along the street at night — or, in some cases, even park their cars by day. People, in brief, have come to fear *one another*. And that, to me, is really frightening.

**WT:** People's attitudes toward violence are a prevailing theme in your recent novel *Psycho House*. Do you think society's attitude towards violence has changed over the course of your career, has become desensitized?

**Bloch:** Of course I think society's attitude towards violence has changed — if only in self-defense. And as, sometimes, the only form of self-defense available in a world where dialing "911" is hardly any guarantee that the police will come, a hard-nosed *bravura* attitude is consciously adopted nowadays, and with predictable results. The "desensitization," as you call it, has become a conscious goal — a sort of psychic vaccination against possible exposure to trauma and terror.

**WT:** You've been quoted in the past as saying that your novel *Psycho* was loosely based on the infamous exploits of Wisconsin murderer Ed Gein. In retrospect, the crimes of Ed Gein seem almost tame compared to the likes of more contemporary killers like Henry Lee Lucas and Richard Ramirez. Do you think the media — news, TV, movies, fiction — have played a significant role in our society's apparent desensitization to violence? Further, do you feel that the creators and purveyors of violence-filled information and/or *entertainment* have a "moral responsibility," in any sense of the phrase? Or is it okay to just throw whatever on the screen or the page and let the audience interpret it as they may.

**Bloch:** I continue to believe that creators and purveyors have an obligation to stand up and be counted. "Self-expression" is not an inherent right in any culture or society if it serves no more purpose than attracting attention through outraging the sensibilities of others. Labeling the purveying of factual material, however gross, as "reporting" is equally hypocritical. Taking no attitude may in itself be the worst attitude of all.

I guess what I'm really talking about is *intention:* Making money, getting noticed, and seeking revenge against real or imaginary enemies seem to me to be the three main reasons, singly or in combination, for genre gross-out. But such motivations are seldom admitted.

**WT:** Speaking of genre gross-out, do you have an opinion on this whole splatterpunk vs. quiet horror debate?

**Bloch:** Yes, both sides talk too much. And I see that I've succumbed to the same temptation.

**WT:** Getting back to your career — how have your goals changed over the course of your career? For example, are you more conscious of imparting a message or theme now than earlier in your career? Or is that more of a subconscious thing, secondary to writing a good *story?*

**Bloch:** I've gone on record in *Who's Who* to address this commonly-asked question, and the answer still stands. "When writing novels such as *Psycho,* my primary purpose is to entertain — but there is nothing which prevents an entertainer from expressing more serious concerns." Note that I refer specifically to novels. There's more room to develop characters through enlargement of their beliefs and opinions than is usually the case in shorter fiction, though at times I've concentrated on this aspect of characterization in short stories if it seems warranted by plot requirements. But I don't consciously subordinate story to message. And — it should also be kept in mind — I don't necessarily share all of the attitudes which some of my characters may expound.

My characters react in accordance with their needs, not mine. Take culinary preferences for example: when writing about a ghoul, one can hardly expect him to recommend the Pritikin Diet.

**WT:** Earlier in your career, you wrote a fair amount of cosmic or Lovecraftian horror — as evidenced by the novel *Strange Eons* and the collection *Mysteries of the Worm.* Do you ever see yourself writing anything of that nature again, or have you gotten the subject out of your system?

Further, do you think such horrors are still relevant/popular to readers today? Or has the focus of horror moved on?

**Bloch:** I don't know myself well enough yet to predict what I may or may not write in the future. If a Lovecraftian idea occurs to me, it's quite possible that I'll put it to paper — though, as was the case with *Strange Eons,* not necessarily in his style of execution. And if I do, I won't be overly concerned about the "relevancy" of my work. It always has been, and always will be, my responsibility to interest the readers and keep them interested.

The present focus doesn't matter, if one adheres to the eternal (and infernal) verities. One may modify style and update approach, but chasing popularity and worrying about "sophistication" is a waste of time. As I write these lines, the most popular and best-known vehicle of fantasy today is something which was first created ninety years ago — *The Phantom of the Opera*.

**WT:** Out of all your past works, are there any in particular that you look at and think, "That was a really good idea, but I wish I'd've written it differently"? If so, which ones?

**Bloch:** I've been a professional writer for fifty-six years now, and out of the umpty-ump short stories, articles, essays, novels, and radio, television, and film scripts, there are scarcely a handful which I'm really satisfied represent the best job I could have done with the material. One keeps learning, or trying to learn, and one refines techniques and approaches. I can evaluate the results only in terms of editorial and reader reaction. As of now, there are perhaps thirty of my short stories which have been reprinted and/or dramatized ten or more times worldwide since they first appeared. "Yours Truly, Jack the Ripper" has been around since 1943 and seems to bear a charmed life; my novel, *Psycho*, has always been in print somewhere during its long career, which began in 1959. I can't quarrel with material which proves itself through perpetuation — even though I certainly feel that there's plenty of room for improvement, and know (or think I know) how I'd go about the job today. The closest thing I can offer by way of an example is my story, "Beetles," as it appears here in this magazine. Contrast

its first incarnation as a short story, in 1938, with its reincarnation as a teleplay in 1986. My plot, although reenacted in a different setting, remains basically the same. The dramatized version benefits by absence of the story's narrator who was, frankly, a cardboard convenience rather than a character. And like the advocates of splatterpunk or quiet horror, he talked too much.

In the more modern teleplay form I could tell the same story with greater economy, while at the same time deliberately retaining the old-fashioned "mummy's curse" theme and approach which was its original inspiration.

What I'm saying is that changes are important to me only if they appear to improve the basic story. I'm not all that interested in being trendy or updating material just to prove I'm still sentient. Changing the title of "Beetles" to "Don't Bug Me" is not necessarily a step in the right direction — any more than trying to capitalize on current interest by calling it "The Phantom of the Coleoptera."

**WT:** Your novel *Psycho House* was published recently, and you're also editing a soon-to-be-released collection entitled *Psycho Paths*. After so many years of having your name invariably associated with *Psycho*, it almost seems as if you're giving in to the stereotype. Is there some such significance to the publication of these two *Psycho*-related books in such short order, or is it just coincidence?

**Bloch:** There may not be any significance in the publication of two *Psycho*-related books in such short order, but there is some insignificance. The anthology you refer to is actually a two-volume anthology of original stories that does not deal with any aspects or characters of my *Psycho* material. I was interested in how various of my colleagues might relate to sociopathic behavior in short stories of their own — and I must say that I've been enormously impressed with their handling of non-supernatural horror. It's my hope that readers will be equally responsive to such insightful work.

As for my own two *Psycho*-related novels, *Psycho II* and *Psycho House,* it's possible they were partially inspired by an attitude of self-defense. Their existence helps prove that I was in no way connected with the films which purported to be sequels to the original.

**WT:** Another "theme" which you've returned to more than once over the years is that of Jack the Ripper. Does the character hold a certain fascination for you, and if so, why?

**Bloch:** Jack the Ripper seems to hold a certain fascination for the general public, a fascination which has endured for over a hundred years. I first became aware of this almost a half-century ago, and wrote the short story previously mentioned. Its own continued existence prompted me to utilize the concept in a variety of ways, as you note. My only personal fascination, however, is in the mystery of the Ripper's identity, which I feel has never been solved. Certainly I'd make no such claim for my fictional "solutions." Perhaps I'm a bit prejudiced in this matter, because over the long years, Jack the Ripper has certainly proven to be a good friend.

In my opinion, anyone who wants to beat Jack the Ripper at his own game certainly has his work cut out for him.

**WT:** Speaking of *Psycho,* Jack the Ripper, and such deranged types: You've been quoted previously as making derogatory comparison of psychotherapy to phrenology (which involved studying the shape of human skulls and bumps on the skull, and making determinations about a person's mental makeup based on this) and further opining that psychotherapy may not be in vogue much longer. Why do you feel this way?

**Bloch:** Phrenology purported to explain human behavior by studying the outside of the skull. Psychotherapy purported to explain human behavior by studying what went on inside the skull. Neither has really succeeded, in my opinion. I believe that discoveries in biochemistry and genetic engineering will further weaken psychotherapeutic claims in terms of diagnosis and treatment.

**WT:** You've spent a fair amount of time imagining the thoughts of unbalanced characters in your stories — don your creative hat for a moment and envision for us a world without psychotherapy: What will take its place?

**Bloch:** The answer seems obvious — computers, of course. We will soon, to all intents and purposes, have mechanical mentors. After which, before most people realize what's happening, we'll have mechanical masters.

**WT:** You've said in the past that movies you saw when you were young, particularly *Phantom of the Opera,* played a big part in starting your writing career. The movie business — or at least the horror movie business — seems to be seriously down in the dumps quality-wise. Have you seen anything lately that you found inspiring or impressive?

**Bloch:** I've seen few recent horror films, and am not qualified to comment on the current output, however profanely.

**WT:** You've been quoted previously as saying — in reference to film studios — that "Reliance on the computer to tell you what to do based on mathematical projections is death to the creative impulse." That quote got me wondering whether you — having obviously spent most of your writing career using pencil and typewriter — have ever become comfortable with computers and word processors? In the same vein, do you think that computers have a negative effect on a writer's creativity?

**Bloch:** A couple of years ago, I dictated four books to a secretary, who in turn put them directly onto a word-processor screen, and thence into a printer. I never became comfortable with these procedures, and aside from bypassing the physical exertion of using a manual typewriter, I still fail to see any advantage in the method.

As to whether or not a writer's creativity is affected, I'd venture it depends to a great extent on the individual writer's mechanical and/or mnemonic-*cum*-mathematical abilities.

Since I don't understand machinery, can't remember even a simple typewriter keyboard arrangement after almost sixty years of usage, and flunked Geometry I, as well as *Nightmare on Elm Street XIV*, there is little hope for me. My best writing is done with a stone tablet and a chisel.

**WT:** You moved to Hollywood in 1959, ostensibly to write for the screen — an occupation you seem to have moved away from in the early '70s. Was that move by choice, and if so, why?

**Bloch**: I went to Hollywood to write for television, then did nine or ten films. I moved away from them as they moved away from me: I had no more desire to work on the type of picture I wouldn't want to see than I'd have for writing stories I wouldn't want to read. Additionally, the passage of a dozen years or so had brought drastic changes in production procedures. The writing of scripts now entailed seeking the approval of a large number of executives, marketing analysts and other experts: I found the notion of working within a "committee system" distasteful. Hollywood was also reaching a point where only about one script out of ten ever actually reached the screen. Incredible as this may seem, many writers made more money working on un-produced screenplays than writers whose work was occasionally filmed. When I realized how much time I'd wasted on efforts which went into turn-around — or wastebaskets — I concentrated on my printed fiction. The "Beetles" script

represented in this magazine was written only to prove to myself that I could still do such work if I wanted to, and wasn't just rationalizing my inability to deliver a suitable effort. Incidentally, I took it on because in this instance there was none of the interference mentioned above: I wrote the script without so much as a single meeting with production people, made no traumatic or dramatic changes or revisions, and encountered no problems whatsoever.

**WT:** You've been quoted in the past as saying that "horror fiction is rapidly reaching a dead end unless there is a revision in structure and concept." Do you still believe that is true?

**Bloch:** Definitely. I'm sure, however, that there are any number of writers who are — and will be — trying to initiate changes for the better in structure and concept. For them, I have only two words — please hurry!

**WT:** You've got a book called *The Jekyll Legacy,* which is a collaboration with Andre Norton. As far as I know, your only previous collaborations were on short stories with Henry Kuttner and Ralph Milne Farley in the '30s. What led you to collaborate once again, and how did it work out?

**Bloch:** It was Andre Norton who proposed we collaborate — and I felt both flattered and honored by the suggestion.

Proceeding as we did — alternating segments of a chapter or so apiece and exchanging them by mail — was an easy procedure. At least it proved to be, for me, because I had the privilege of working with one of the finest talents in the field of fantasy, whose gifts of characterization and detailed knowledge of the period background we dealt with greatly enriched the story.

As to how it worked out, the answer will probably be apparent before this interview has reached publication.

**WT:** What else do you have forthcoming? What are you currently working on?

**Bloch:** There are several things forthcoming, or should be in the near future. I'm told that one of my short stories, "Almost Human," will be a part of an anthology film, *Tales from the Darkside II.* I've also been informed that another of my stories, "The Final Performance," will be produced as a one-act play incorporated in a new theatrical version of the celebrated *Grand Guignol.* In addition to the two-volume anthology I'm editing for early publication, I currently have an autobiography in the hands of my agent in New York. It is my intention to go on living it until the last chapter. And maybe I can come up with a surprise ending.

Ω

# THERE ARE NO GHOSTS IN CATHOLIC SPAIN

There are no ghosts in Catholic Spain.
What, none?
None! Nil!
It runs uphill against the grain of their religion.
In any region you might go
The rain in Spain falls on a ghostless plain.
On jaunts about Castille you'll find it so:
No haunts!
Those castles, ruined, empty-jawed, where gaunts
In England's guilt-prone nights might sprout,
In Spain are only filled with cat-footfalls of rain.
The papal architects have planned them out.
No ghosts are manufactured to weep here
Through doleful month or suffering year.
The dead, the good/bad church's dead?
(Learn it well.)
Jump straight to heaven! Bang!
Or:
Go to hell!

*No Loitering,* says Mother Church.
No reconnoitering on Earth's front porch.
Up you go: Angel's wings!
Down you go: Torch!
No ectoplasm whispering cold mirrors: "Alas!"
Pausing to admire

Its skull-face in the glass.
Up you jump: Cherub's breath!
Down you fall: Fire!
Not here: O, Lazarus, quit tomb, come forth!
He's long since blown north
On pagan winds toward colder climes.
Westminster's chimes do beckon him
To reckon with pale Protestants who boast
No English moat lacks skeletons,
Each tower? gives midnight snacks to ghost.
Gah, let the fools maunder!
Let their cold bods wander,
Lost in their own sleep,
Raking the rats awake and awash in the wainscot,
Making the old moldy flesh of lost London cold-creep,
Doubtful of heaven, uncertain of flames.
Let Hamlet's sire dropkick lost Yorick's skull downstairs
In winless games
For what gain?
Better the Catholic hush of soundless rain
Which falls in Spain upon a ghostless plain,
Where only the wind walks battlements
To touch and toll God's bell.
Again:
Good souls? To heaven!
Bad?
Go to hell.

— **Ray Bradbury**

# TAP DANCING

## by John Gregory Betancourt

Martha Peckinpah sat alone in the back of the theater, watching a dress rehearsal for *Stardust Whammy*. Floodlights bathed the stage in silvers and blues, glittering the sparkle-sewn tuxedos on both dancers. Moog-synthesized Brahms swelled to dizzying peaks as the men rat-tat-tatted to a stop.

*Brilliant.* That's what the critics would say, Martha thought. Only she knew better. There hadn't been anything new or fresh in the choreography, and the kid on the left had been a half-beat slow on at least a dozen of his repartees. But nobody else had noticed. Standards had fallen, and tap had died a lingering death. This revival was the best she'd seen in the last five years, though, and it might last all of a week before closing. She felt a hollowness inside as she thought of how television and movies and glittery, shallow theatrics like *Cats* had replaced dance and theater as *the* American performing arts.

But the house lights would be coming on in a minute and the dancers might see her. She had to hurry. If the manager caught her again —

It would be: *Miss Peckinpah, you know you can't come in here and bother people. You'll make the dancers nervous.* Or: *Don't you ever learn? If you don't leave, I'll have to call the police. Again.* Or, if he was in a kind mood: *Miss Peckinpah, sneaking in during rehearsals isn't proper. I know you used to dance here — but that was forty years ago, for crying out loud. Things have changed. You're no longer a star.*

Pity. That was the worst. If it hadn't been for the car crash —

Shuddering, she seized her silver-handled cane and levered herself from the seat, cursing under her breath. Her left knee buckled. The dress she wore, with its faded cherry-blossom print, tangled around her like some monstrous python.

She grabbed for the chair in front of her — and missed. Teetering, arms flailing, she fell. Sharp, fiery pain shot through her left leg. She pressed hands to mouth and managed to stifle her cry . . . thankfully what noise trickled out sounded more like the whimper of some distant, wounded animal than the shriek of a woman in agony.

Carefully she eased forward. Grabbing her purse, she searched for her pain pills. She found the bottle and ripped off its cap, only to have her shaking hand scatter the contents across the floor. Pills tap-tap-tapped downhill toward the stage.

The lights began to brighten. Her leg throbbed. *No time.* Bending, she ducked down and prayed nobody would see her.

The dancers walked up the aisle, laughing and joking, the little steel taps on their shoes muffled by the worn red carpet. The manager and two stagehands followed, muttering gloomily about potential box office. She pressed her eyes shut and held her breath. At last the doors squeaked and she was alone.

*Why me, oh God why me?* In a rare moment of introspection it struck her how pathetic she must seem, a crazy old woman nobody remembered, sneaking into theaters just to criticize the young, just to say to herself, *Oh, how much greater we were back then.* Better she had never come back to this theater.

Better she had died in that car crash forty years before. Better she had never been born.

"Not so." It was a soft voice, a man's voice, and the words held a strange inflection — a trace of a southern accent, and something else, something more.

"Who said that?" she called.

"I did."

She became aware of light — a soft bluegray glow that seemed to surround her. A man dressed all in black leather sat beside her. He had shoulder-length black hair and wore dark glasses, an old-fashioned pair with round lenses and wire rims. A silver cross dangled from his left ear. He smiled and there was an aliveness about him that surprised her.

"You're not Mr. Lipshitz, the manager," Martha said. "You can't throw me out —"

"Did I say I wanted to?"

"No." There was something naggingly familiar about him, she thought. She'd seen him before, somewhere. Perhaps on television?

"I'm just a visitor. If you need a name, Johnny will do."

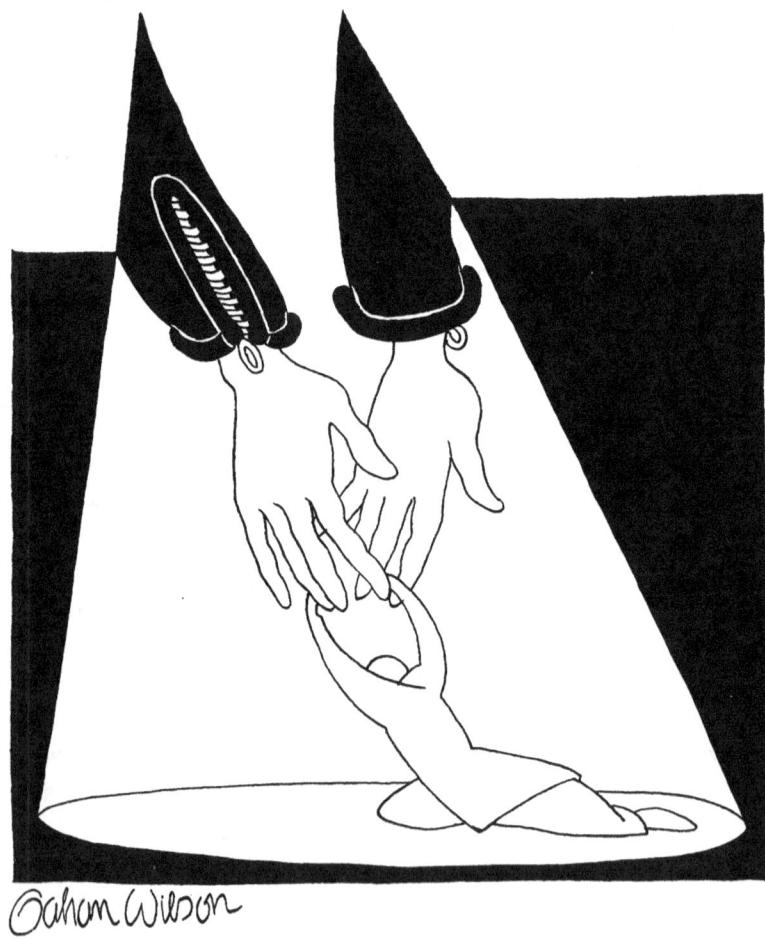

"Can you help me up?"

"If that's what you want, yes." He took her hand — his touch was cool, his grip strong — and he pulled her to her feet with little effort. The pain in Martha's leg seemed gone. She stood with no trouble for the first time since her accident.

"Who — what?"

"Did you like their dance?" he asked softly.

"It could have been better."

He shook his head slowly. "And what are you going to do to fix it?"

"Me?"

"Why not you?"

"Son, I'm old, and I'm sick, and I don't have time for this nonsense. They don't have the talent. They're not as good as we were, that's all there is to it."

"You're right, of course. A big star like you — I should just let you go on about your life. Whatever it is. Whatever it's worth."

Martha winced. "You're cruel," she whispered.

"I used to watch your movies," he continued. "You and Fred, you were the best. It's a shame to let all that go to waste. I *know*. It's too late for me — I never shared my gifts, I hoarded them — and now I've got to work to make up for it. There's a balance. You get some, you share some. Don't hide it all away. There's so much you know, so much you can still *do* —"

"Don't lecture me!" she said. "I don't need your pity!" She couldn't make herself look at him. Guilt? Did she feel . . . *guilt?* "That was such a long time ago."

"Have you forgotten?"

Had she forgotten? She could have laughed. *Had she forgotten?* Of course not. She couldn't forget, not ever. Tap had been her whole life. Nothing else had mattered. Until those screaming brakes, that tree rushing at her —

"Please," he said, taking her hand, squeezing it reassuringly. "Dance with me?"

"What do you mean?" She finally met his gaze. There was hope there, and faith. He knew she could dance — he remembered!

"Come," he said. He took her elbow gently and led her down to the stage. She was halfway there before she noticed she wasn't using her cane.

"I left my —" she began.

"Do you need it?" he asked.

"No. No!" She said it with conviction, then laughed. "No!" She stepped ahead of him, courage and confidence welling up inside her. Her stride was jaunty. The years seemed to be melting away. She could see the theater as it had once been: the red velvet seats, the plush carpeting, the crowds —

Then somehow she was on the stage. The lights shone bright and hot like always, like she'd never been away. She felt a heady rush of elation. Then she looked down, saw her scarred, treelike legs jutting out, those old woman's legs with their sagging muscles —

"Oh no!" she cried.

"It doesn't matter," Johnny said.

And he was right, it didn't. Martha took a deep breath. Suddenly she was no longer old Martha Peckinpah but Desiree Diamond again — star of stage and screen. She'd danced with the best of them, Fred Astaire, Gene Kelly, Ray Bolger —

Tap-tap-tap. *Rat-ta-ta-*tap-*ta-tap*. Her feet moved on their own. They remembered. The opening number from *Broadway Bound* —

Johnny now wore a black tux with tails. He took her hand, spun her slowly, and they moved into all the old dances, up and across the stage, tapping away, faster and faster, around and around and around. Her red silk dress swirled. The tails of his tux whipped by. Martha was laughing and tears streamed down her face like they would never stop. Around and around and around they went, and the orchestra played as though their lives depended on it. *Tap-a-tap-ratta-tap-tap!*

Martha came to a stop, quivering. Her breath came in short gasps. She looked down. Her faded dress with its cherry-blossom print had returned. Johnny, smiling, gave her a little bow.

"You haven't forgotten," he said.

"No," she agreed, "I haven't."

"Then I thank you," he said, turning to go. "Thank you, and goodbye."

"Wait!" Martha called. She took a step and the pain shot through her leg. She gasped, stumbled.

Johnny paused. "I'm sorry. I can't stay any longer."

"But *why?*" she cried.

"Purgatory isn't a place, it's a process. You have to work off your debt." Then he turned and hopped down from the stage, melting off into the darkness. His voice seemed to carry back like an echo of an echo. *"Remember . . ."*

By the time Martha reached the aisle, the theater was deserted.

She limped back to her apartment and collapsed in her overstuffed armchair, all her shattered dreams coming back to haunt her. *Broadway Bound,* closed in mid-run because of her accident. Her canceled contract with Sam Goldwyn. All her ruined plans.

A tear traced a path down the creases of her cheek. Angrily she brushed it away. *I don't owe them anything,* she thought. *They never came to see me. They never wrote. They just swept me under the carpet and kept going with their lives like nothing had happened, nothing had changed.*

She stabbed the remote control with one finger. The television flickered to life.

And she found herself looking at Johnny's face.

"— dead tonight, Johnny Devlin, head singer of the heavy metal rock group, Cruel Blade. A drug overdose is suspected, and an autopsy has been or-

dered. Fans are already mourning Johnny's loss. Cruel Blade's first album, a groundbreaking mix of heavy metal, jazz, and reggae, is currently topping the charts in both the U.S. and England —"

Martha hurriedly flicked the television off. Johnny's words came back to her, and she shuddered. *That's the way of things when you're working off your debt.*

Martha poured herself a brandy, downed it, had a second. Her hands were shaking again. *You get some, you share some.*

She spent a sleepless night wondering.

The next morning, bright and early, she donned her good dress — the one she always wore to funerals — and had another drink. Then, spirit girded, she set off for the theater.

Rather than sliding her trusty old butter knife into the firedoor's lock, lifting the latch, and sneaking in the way she usually did, she went straight to the stage entrance.

Adam Lipshitz, the manager, saw her coming and came out to meet her. "For the thousandth time, Miss Peckinpah," he began, "I don't want you coming here and —"

Martha cut him off with a curt gesture. "I watched the show last night. Your dancers are good this time, Lipshitz. Really good. But their routines stink."

"I choreographed it myself!"

She snorted. "It shows! You need a professional. How long till opening? A week?"

He nodded.

"Then there's still time . . ." She smiled, and focused on him once more. "I want to help you," she said kindly, in her best grandmotherly voice. "I think this time you could really have something here, something important, something *great* instead of merely adequate.

Will you let me restage the routines for you?"

"Why should I listen to you?"

"I'm the best."

"You *were* the best."

"I still am," she said. "I still remember . . ."

"How much will it cost?" he asked, eyes narrowing.

"You really don't understand, do you? I'm an old woman. I don't need more than I already have. This isn't for *money*, Lipshitz, it's for *art*. For *tap*. That's why you couldn't get it right."

He threw up his hands. "Okay, already! It doesn't hurt to look. Come in, I'll get the dancers. Then we'll see what you suggest."

Martha followed him, cane tap-tap-tapping the way to the stage. She began to smile. Backstage, with the smell of makeup, with the tiny dressing rooms and the clutter of props — it felt like coming home. How long had it been? Too long.

And when Lipshitz opened the curtain onto the side of the stage, when she saw the dancers fumbling their way through routines that should have come like water flowing down a river, she finally knew that this was good, this was right. Perhaps she'd been meant for this in the cosmic order of things. Perhaps her accident had happened merely to guide her here, to this particular moment, to make her a director instead of a star.

When *Stardust Whammy* opened, it would be magic, it would be art, and it would be beauty.

And she knew she'd be happy for the first time in forty years.

"This is for you, Johnny," she whispered. "Thank you . . . I *do* remember."

Ω

# POEM WRITTEN ON A TRAIN JUST LEAVING A SMALL SOUTHERN TOWN

Druid City, Druid City, what a pity, what a shame,
Until noon of April 16th, I had never heard your name.
Is the all of you a forest, is the sum of you deep wood?
After midnight, then, what happens in your gnarled oak neighborhood?
Alabama is your mater is your pater, yonder oak?
Did you wander here from Memphis or from Celtic Roanoke?
That's if Roanoke was Celtic, and if not, then where and when
Did a shambling host of chestnuts plant you here in rainfall glen?
Just this side of Tuscaloosa, did the syrup: Pepper/Coke
Drown your acorns, spout your rootlings high in mobs of elm and oak?
Do your priests survive in traffic, evil cops on every beat?
Do their acolytes teach sapling-innocents in every street?
Does your secret population rise at twilight, shunning sun?
Were they here before the pilgrims, centuries before Bull Run?
Druid City, Alabama, was your mama mystic fen?
Did the village smithy shape you with his devil's anvils — when?
In that anvil chorus forest, were the natives scrawny, few?
Was your natal flora fatal, rank persimmon, morbid yew?
Was the raping of the Sabines carried out in centaur deeps
Where, in central Alabama, Alexander, map Pope, sleeps?
True or untrue, glad to see you, gladder still to see you gone;
Druid City, rainfalled, misting . . . sunk in locomotive dawn.

— **Ray Bradbury**

# ONE MORE STORY TO TELL

## excerpts from an unauthorized autobiography
## by Robert Bloch

At the time I acquired my first copy, *Weird Tales* was scarcely a household name, and during the thirty-odd years of the magazine's existence it never became one. And despite posthumous fame many of those who wrote about it later referred to the publication as *Wierd Tales*. In today's drug culture it's *Wired Tales*.

Come to think of it, to many people this last title might have seemed accurate enough, even in 1937 when my own readership began.

The cover story which attracted my attention at that time illustrated a serial which dealt with an ancient Egyptian city still flourishing today directly below Chicago, unbeknownst even to Al Capone.

In issues to come I read the adventures of a French physician and amateur detective whose monthly confrontations with the supernatural occurred aboveground. Every thirty days he staked out a vampire, neutered a werewolf, exorcised a demon, or laid a ghost — the latter procedure, in those days, was nonsexual. All these activities took place on the streets and in the dwellings of Harrisonville, N.J., a community which seemed to be inhabited by almost as many monsters as Beverly Hills. It took me several years to learn that the city of Harrisonville was a fictitious creation, and several more to discover that the same thing was true of Beverly Hills.

But by far the most horrifying concept, and to me the most convincing, was an account of ghouls feasting in their burrows below the cemeteries and subways of modern Boston. The story, "Pickman's Model," was credited to one H.P. Lovecraft, and I made a mental note to remember both the title and the name of the author.

This is neither the time nor the place to go into the publishing history of what its masthead first described to be "The Unique Magazine" and then as "A Magazine of the Bizarre and Unusual." It was all these things and more; to me personally *Weird Tales* became a sort of nontheological *Book of Revelation*. What it revealed was that fantastic fiction was not necessarily the work of long-deceased authors like Poe, Hawthorne or de Maupassant; its prose and poetry were not entombed in pages from the past. Death was alive and well and living in Chicago.

To be exact, its present address was 840 N. Michigan Avenue. Here *Weird Tales* maintained editorial offices, but not quite as well as I then imagined. Although the magazine never expired, a lot of its subscriptions did. Battling circulation problems, the publication seemed chronically moribund and constantly hooked up to a life-support system on which creditors kept threatening to pull the plug.

All this, of course, I learned much later. Living in the suburbs of Chicago made it difficult to venture into the downtown Loop on my own, and it never entered my mind to seek out the lair where monsters lurked, whether as gangsters aboveground or as Egyptians below.

What my parents though of my taste

remains unclear to me. Although they seemed disinterested in reading my favorite magazine they offered no objections to cover illustrations of damsels in various stages of distress and undress, and continued to supply me with quarters for the monthly issues. Their own preferences were *The Saturday Evening Post, Liberty Magazine, The Literary Digest* and *The Ladies' Home Journal,* none of which specialized in the supernatural. Once in a while my mother purchased a copy of a magazine called *Harper's Bazaar* but if there was a periodical called *Harper's Bizarre,* I never got to see it.

Nor did I see the byline of H.P. Lovecraft anywhere except in the pages of *Weird Tales.* Bookstore clerks couldn't place his name, public libraries had never heard of him, school teachers — when I tried explaining the sort of thing he wrote — didn't want to.

It took years before I learned the background of my favorite writer of horror fiction. Again, this is not the time or place to delve into details, nor is it necessary. Today biographical material on Lovecraft and critical evaluations of his efforts abound, and most of his work remains in print.

Sufficient to say that Howard Phillips Lovecraft was born in Providence, R.I. in 1890 and, with the exception of a brief residence in New York during his marriage in the mid-Twenties, lived there throughout his life. Of long-time New England stock, his parents were short-lived, and both suffered from mental illness in their latter years. Judged a sickly child by his mother, Lovecraft was removed from school, but his phenomenal precocity aided him in an impressive self-education. As a young man he dabbled in writing — articles, essays, poetry and short fantasies in prose contributed to the field of amateur journalism. A dwindling income from a small family inheritance and the necessity of helping support two spinster aunts forced him to turn his talents towards professional markets which published fantasy and supernatural horror fiction.

Such markets proved few and far between. In fact the only consistent outlet for the outré was *Weird Tales* itself. Lovecraft wrote and sold what he could of his own work and did revisions and ghostwriting for others, but he never rose above the poverty-level, nor surfaced to general recognition or critical acclaim. Only a very few of his stories found publication outside the pages of *Weird Tales,* and even there a number were rejected.

In a professional career spanning a mere fifteen years he gradually graduated from the early, abbreviated poetic prose into longer — though sometimes equally lurid — tales of horror. Then, about the time I discovered him, he began a cycle of stories loosely-linked to a common background; a cosmos of his own creation based on what has become known as the "Cthulhu Mythos."

His vision of a universe ruled by monstrous entities which once claimed earth as their own had a persuasive paranoid logic. Lovecraft, himself a strict materialist, bridged the gap between fantasy and reality by the introduction of modern science in many of these tales. Hidden horrors were hinted at by scholars, researchers, astronomers and astrophysicists, hunted down by teams of explorers using the resources of contemporary technology.

It was with these tales that Lovecraft came into his own. "The Call of Cthulhu," "The Dunwich Horror," "The Whisperer in Darkness," "At the Mountains of Madness," "The Shadow Out of Time" — these, plus a half dozen others, form the basis of an enduring concept. Enduring, and endearing to literally dozens of other writers who have since borrowed Lovecraft's Mythos, monsters, and in many cases, mannerisms of style and presentation. Some of them made use of his imaginary New England locales, including Dunwich, Innsmouth, Kingsport, and the city of Arkham. The latter is the home of Miskatonic University, which owns a translation of the *Necronomicon*. This is the source-book for Mythos lore and the spells and incantations that can presumably conjure up or cast down its immortal monstrosities.

Lovecraft had a lot of fun inventing the Mythos, but some of the succeeding generations of readers tended to take it more seriously. References to Cthulhu have been incorporated into the rituals of several cults, and years ago a few unscrupulous dealers in rare books claimed to actually possess copies of the *Necronomicon*.

I imagine all this might have amused Lovecraft, as well as helping to confirm his views regarding intellectual and cultural decadence of modern society. As a result of both physical and financial limitations his travels and social context were curtailed. He communicated with the outside world largely through correspondence so widespread and voluminous as to be almost legendary. And it was in letters that he created a legendary persona; that of a New England gentleman displaced in Time. Pen in hand and tongue in cheek, he proclaimed himself a Tory, a loyal subject of His Majesty, King George III. He frequently affected the grammar and spelling of colonial days and began referring to himself as an elderly person while still in his thirties.

He was, in reality, a kind, considerate, courteous man, generous to a fault with his time and talent. Since his death more than half a century ago Lovecraft and his work have been both revered and reviled. But two facts remain indisputable. Professionally, his influence on the field of supernatural horror fiction was equal to that of Edgar Allan Poe; personally, he was one of the last true gentlemen.

Mind you, back in 1927 I didn't know all that much about either Lovecraft or *Weird Tales*, and probably wouldn't have cared if I did. What mattered to me was that this guy wrote good stuff in a swell magazine.

In school I was forced to squirm my way through the works of Oliver Wendell Holmes, James Lowell, and Henry Wadsworth Longfellow.

In "Pickman's Model," the ghouls ate all three.

Now that, I decided, was poetic justice. And I still think so today.

The apartment building in which we dwelt after we moved to Milwaukee was bordered by an alley just one block long, ending at the street to our north. This poorly-paved stretch was flanked on the east by the backyards of other apartment buildings and the trash bins of their occupants. Standing beside the bins were long lines of garbage cans that served as condominiums for flies.

The west side of the alley offered a rear view of the local movie theater, which didn't look all that good from the front, either. Adjoining it was a massive soot-blackened structure which had once been a brewery; now, during the years of Prohibition, it had become a dairy. How they trained the cows to stop giving beer and produce milk instead is something I never knew.

During winter the alley was a wind tunnel; in summer it became a heat-retaining inferno. But for one day on or about the first of each month, the alleyway was transformed for me into a path to paradise.

At the far end of the alley was Ogden Avenue, and there, directly across the street, was the Ogden Smoke Shop. Despite its name, the shop didn't sell any smoke, although it was possible to purchase cigars, cigarettes, pipe tobacco and assorted merchandise from two elderly spinster ladies. I never learned to identify them; for all I know, their names could have been Nieman and

Marcus. But that didn't matter to me. What was important is that they also stocked magazines. And one of the magazines they sold was *Weird Tales*.

It was after our move to 620 East Knapp Street that I resumed my perusal of this periodical on a regular basis. Despite the economic effect of the Depression, *Weird Tales* still cost 25 cents, but that was one of the facts (or figures) of life I had to live with. Most drugstores and newsstands didn't bother to handle this exorbitantly-priced pulp magazine; the Ogden Smoke Shop was just about the only place where I could purchase the current issue. And purchase I must, because it was impossible to just stand there and consume the entire contents of the magazine with one or both of the shop's proprietors plunging their ocular daggers into my back. The message was clear; I had better buy because they would spare me no quarter.

In keeping with my exalted position as a high school student, my parents maintained me on the allowance of, roughly, a dollar a month. This sum I was permitted to squander as I saw fit, on sodas, candy, carfare, movie tickets and designer drugs of my choice. By cutting down on my consumption of carbohydrates, borrowing streetcar passes and confining motion picture attendance to nights when tickets were ten or fifteen cents, I managed to keep the necessary quarter in reserve for the next issue of *Weird Tales*.

But that didn't completely solve my problem. The anonymous ladies who ran the shop (could they have been Emma and Lizzie Borden, I wonder?) only ordered two copies of the magazine each month. This meant I had to get mine before the supply was exhausted, even if I exhausted myself in the process, which was usually the case.

On the morning which marked the first of each month — or the second, if the first happened to fall on a Sunday — I would roll out of bed promptly at six-thirty. I dressed quickly and sneaked out quietly. Whatever the weather, I took the shortcut up the alley and usually reached the door of the shop just as it was being unlocked. Sometimes I even lugged in the bundles of magazines which had been dumped there, the sooner to stake my claim.

Many times I mused upon the possibility of sparing myself all this time, effort, and stress by subscribing to the magazine instead of making individual monthly purchases. For $2.50 a year *Weird Tales* would be delivered directly to my door, and I'd be saving a whole half-dollar per annum, if you'll pardon the expression. But what if an issue got lost in the mail? What if some other resident of our building stole a copy from the downstairs mailbox? And, not to put too fine a point upon it, just where the Hell would I get $2.50 together at one time in order to take out a subscription?

Matters of high finance were always a problem. There was an interlude during which my monthly purchases of the magazine ceased. But though I told myself I'd sworn off (as I later did in regards to LSD, PCP, AT&T and other recreational drugs) I was still hooked.

In particular, my addiction to the work of H.P. Lovecraft increased. By the time I resumed reading *Weird Tales* his output had slowed, frequently leaving me frantic for a fix.

In the letter column of the magazine long-time readers frequently referred to Lovecraft's stories which had seen publication long ago and had not been reprinted. As far as I knew, none of his work appeared in book-form although two of his efforts had received honorable mentions in annual anthologies purporting to represent the best short stories of the year. A fair number of back issues were still available from the publisher at cover-price, but few contained the titles I was searching for. A Lovecraft junkie, I was hungry for more highs. What could I do?

As it has so frequently during a long lifetime, sheer stupidity came to my rescue. I sat down and — using the Palmer Method of Penmanship which I haven't mastered to this day — scrawled out a letter to Mr. Lovecraft c/o the magazine. Identifying myself as an ardent fan (and a brash, presumptuous teen-age idiot) I inquired if he might inform me as to where I could locate some of his stories presently out of print.

There came a time, some years later, when I myself received similar letters from readers or would-be readers. Invariably I replied, advising them to drop dead, get stuffed, or save on funeral expenses by willing their bodies to a cannibal.

Fortunately for me, Mr. Lovecraft proved to be far more charitable. There was nothing in his nature to sour the milk of human kindness. Within a remarkably short time I received a reply from 10 Barnes Street in Providence, Rhode Island.

In his minute, distinctive calligraphy (penned by a method unbeknownst to Palmer) the writer informed me that he and his two maiden aunts were in the process of packing and moving to a new address, 66 College Street. He had just finished taking inventory of his magazine stories and book collection, and was enclosing copies of both. If there were any stories on the list which I wanted to read he would be happy to lend me tearsheets. If there were any books in his library which might interest me he would be glad to lend me his copies.

To state that this response had a traumatic effect on me is to put it mildly, not to say tritely. The notion that a full-fledged adult literary celebrity would make such an offer to a half-fledged teen-age nonentity was as astonishing to me as it was commonplace to Lovecraft.

Needless to say I jumped at the offer after first hurdling the problems of

postage and parental approval. I never borrowed any books but I did solicit a loan of such stories as "The Rats in the Walls," "The Outsider," and "The Picture in the House." Formerly a Lovecraft fan, I was now a Lovecraft devotee.

More significantly, I had become a regular correspondent with the man who variously referred to himself as "Grandpa Theobald" or "The Old Gentleman," he having reached the venerable age of forty-two at the time. I had also thus unwittingly become a member of what was later styled the Lovecraft Circle — a group of friends and fans, many of whom were themselves writers or aspired to be.

Soon Lovecraft introduced me to some of them by mail, including such well-known *Weird Tales* writers as Clark Ashton Smith, Henry S. Whitehead, E. Hoffman Price and August W. Derleth. Smith, a poet, artist and sculptor, wrote stories which many readers compared favorably to Lovecraft's; he lived in faraway California and we never met. Whitehead had been an Episcopal minister in the West Indies whose fantasy fiction frequently dealt with voodoo and similar beliefs; he died soon after we conducted our brief correspondence. E. Hoffman Price saw military service in the Philippines, France and Mexico; an expert swordsman, an orientalist and astrologer, he lived eighty-nine full years. August W. Derleth, who later discarded his middle initial, was a poet, critic, essayist, budding novelist and near-neighbor; his home was Sauk City, Wisconsin, a hundred and twenty miles west of me, as the crow flies. But owing to governmental deregulation of birds the crows weren't flying all that often in 1933. It would be several years before we met face to face, and even then I travelled by Greyhound instead of crow.

It was much easier for me to journey via streetcar to see another Lovecraft friend, a gentleman named Maurice W. Moe who taught English at West Division High School. The idea of a student visiting a teacher in his family home was in itself rather heady stuff at the time, as was corresponding with grown-up fans like Bernard Austin Dwyer and J. Vernon Shea, Jr.

There were perhaps a dozen other members of the Circle; with a few I had peripheral contact, others I met years later or not at all. But I learned quite a bit about most of them and a great deal more about Lovecraft himself — whom they commonly referred to as "HPL."

Lack of funds generally prevented him from travelling, so many of his friendships were made and maintained by mail. Diurnal duties included his own ventures into prose or poetry and all-too-underpaid ghost-writing or rewriting the work of others. Nocturnally, chronic insomnia aided and abetted his devotion to correspondence. The length and literacy of his letters are legendary; five thick volumes of them have been selected and published, representing only a tiny fraction of his output. If he'd diverted that time and effort to tales instead of the mails, fantasy literature would be the richer.

But people like myself would be the poorer. One of HPL's stories was titled *The Silver Key,* and a sequel — written in collaboration with E. Hoffman Price — was "Through the Gates of the Silver Key." In these stories Lovecraft himself appears as a character named Randolph Carter, whose silver key unlocks the gates of dreams.

To me those two tales and their titles came to assume a personal and particular significance, for it was Lovecraft who gave me a key and opened a doorway to my dreams. Quite early in our correspondence HPL suggested I might be interested in trying my own hand at writing with an eye to publication. A quick inventory of physical assets confirmed that I did indeed possess a hand and an eye, plus backups. And since Lovecraft's suggestion generously in-cluded his willingness to inspect my efforts, what more did I need?

Talent, ideas, and experience, for starters. In the absence of all three, I unwittingly elected to follow in Lovecraft's footsteps — a route since chosen by dozens of future *fantasiastes.* Lacking a style of my own, I imitated HPL's; devoid of original concepts, my sketchy plots were, to put it charitably, derivative; as for experience, hadn't I written a school project, a short piece about life in the future, when I was only eleven years old? Surely now, having survived to become sixteen, I ought to have the ability to toss off five hundred or even a thousand words of master-pieces like "The Madness of Lucian Gray."

Effusions of this sort, which should have been tossed off directly into the wastebasket, I sent off to my literary mentor. If he discovered grammatical or factual errors he offered gentle correction. I must have perpetrated four or five such pieces over as many months, in return for which he offered encouragement instead of criticism. And encouragement was precisely what I needed. Early on, at HPL's instigation I sent one of my efforts to August Derleth, whose reaction was not quite as favorable. To put it bluntly — and he did — Derleth told me flat out that I would never become a professional writer.

As a matter of fact, it was to take eleven more years before my first hard-cover book collection of short stories was published — by August Derleth.

But I anticipate, which is something I could scarcely do back then in the early months of 1934. By this time, again at HPL's suggestion, I'd sent several stories to William L. Crawford, a printer who aspired to become a publisher. In the faraway metropolis of Everett, Pennsylvania, he produced digest-sized magazines which featured a number of professional writers but paid zilch for contributions. Crawford, having nothing to lose, put my first story into print in 1934; its title was "Lilies" and the periodical was called *Marvel Tales.* Another of his short-lived publications, *Unusual Stories,* brought out something which I christened "The Black Lotus."

While Crawford had nothing to lose, it turned out I had little to gain. The so-called magazines bore little or no resemblance to anything found on the newsstands or even produced from under the overcoats of pornography-peddlers, where their wares were concealed in that puritanical period. Showing copies of these crudely-printed periodicals around would scarcely serve to establish my credentials as a "published" writer. Meanwhile, back at the school, I was still struggling to learn how to type properly. And time was running out; that last postgraduate semester had almost ended.

Then, all too suddenly it did end, with both a bang and a whimper. The bang came from an all-night graduation party, and the whimper came from me.

Okay, I was seventeen years old, a high school graduate, and that just about summed it up. I owned one suit, an extra jacket, a hat, two pairs of worn-down shoes and a rundown watch. I had no job, no prospect of getting one, and no aptitude or special skills to offer.

To tell the truth, I was beginning to feel somewhat guilty about rejecting that university scholarship. After all, my mother had been a grammar school teacher before she entered social work, and my father spoke highly of higher education. Undoubtedly both of them would have been pleased if I had chosen to obtain a degree and to into a teaching career; pleased, and in those deepest and darkest days of the Depression, probably relieved concerning my future.

But right now I didn't have any future. All I had was a somewhat willful and stubborn conviction which, after taking a deep breath I conveyed to them directly.

"If you want to be a writer, give it a try," my father said.

"It's your life. You must do what you think best," my mother told me.

I was greatly relieved, but I should have expected those answers. When the Prohibition law was repealed, I joined various of my older postgraduate friends in sampling alcoholic pleasures. These experiments culminated in an epic binge with a classmate which resulted in a lifelong distaste for gin. More immediately, it resulted in a burst of parental disapproval. My mother made it plain to me that she didn't want her son to win a gold medal at the Olympics for diving into a drunk tank. And yet on my following birthday, one of my gifts was a pint of whiskey — from my mother. It was her way of letting me know that I was responsible for my own actions and that she had faith in me.

This attitude on the part of my parents never faltered, and as a result I seldom faltered either. Once I completed the summit meeting concerning my plans for the future, the next step was comparatively easy. I'd accumulated a few dollars as graduation gifts from Chicago relatives; with them I purchased a secondhand typewriter and a secondhand card table and thus set up shop in a corner of my bedroom. Unable to find a source of used carbons and secondhand typing paper, I boldly rushed down to the nearest Woolworth's and purchased close to a dollar's worth of this material, together with several manila envelopes. For approximately twenty-two dollars I had assembled a complete armamentarium with which to wage a war against poverty, and now, all I had to do was write.

I trained my sights on the most obvious and visible target, *Weird Tales.* Instead of bombarding them with contributions, I took careful aim before shooting off a story in their direction. This cautious approach didn't reflect any particular intelligence on my part.

What it demonstrated was that in addition to teaching myself how to write I also had to teach myself how to type properly at the same time.

The secondhand card table was rickety and at times its legs seemed ready to give way as I pounded the machine it supported. The secondhand machine wasn't all that spry either — as a matter of fact, I believe it was one of the first typewriters William Shakespeare ever used — and frequently its keys jammed and the carriage lever had a miscarriage.

Words are weapons, too. Assembling several thousand of them, I constructed a story called "The Secret in the Tomb," which was a real bomb.

From what I later learned, many hundreds of such bombs were dropped every month upon the desk of the magazine's sole editor and reader. Since the magazine published a mere dozen or so stories in each issue, most of the bombs were effective only in exploding the hopes of their writers.

Why a battle-scarred veteran of long-time literary warfare would notice the feeble dud I delivered remains a mystery to this day. But in July 1934, six weeks after graduating from high school, I received a letter of acceptance for my story. I would be recompensed at the standard rate, a penny a word, which added up to the substantial sum of $20.

Even though payment would not be made until publication, in six short weeks I had already earned back all but $2 of my reckless initial investment towards a career.

More important to me was the fact that I had suddenly and almost miraculously become a professional writer, a contributor to the very magazine which published the work of my favorite author and present pen-pal. On the day the letter of acceptance was received I informed my parents, and sent off word to Lovecraft. Then, as visions of megabucks danced in my head, I sat down and started to write another story.

In the five-month period that followed I sold four stories for a grand total of $100. If I could keep up the pace during the twelve months thereafter and write longer pieces, I might escalate my income to as much as $300 a year.

Of course this wouldn't be a sufficient amount to make me totally self-supporting, but then I was never any good at mathematics. All I knew is if I could step up my output, perhaps in five or six years I'd make enough money to starve to death.

Quickly writing (and selling) that second story turned out to be a good idea. "The Feast in the Abbey" was five hundred words longer and a smidge better than its predecessor. The editor decided to use it as my first appearance in the magazine, and this proved providential. It attracted enough favorable comment in the letter column to take the curse off my own letter which appeared several months before I became a published writer. In it, as a fan and reader, I had taken somewhat humorous but unmistakable exception to a character called Conan the Barbarian, hero of a series of stories written by Robert E. Howard. Mr. Howard was also a correspondent of Lovecraft's and had written many other tales which I admired, but I found Conan much too barbaric for my tastes.

Mr. Howard and his barbarous creation had many partisans, all of whom waited in ambush for my debut. Like Conan himself they were equally adept with broadswords or bludgeons, led by a gentleman whose surname, appropriately enough, was Anger.

Using missives as missiles they skewered me for my opinion and the even more heinous crime of criticizing a fellow-author. The fact that my letter appeared in an earlier issue, when I was still a fan, didn't save my neck. I believe execution was avoided only because that second story of mine was printed first.

Had the other preceded it, the Conanites might well have argued that anyone who wrote that badly himself had no right to censure the work of his peers. But somehow my story saved me from such a verdict and the literary lynching which might have followed.

It also taught me a valuable lesson. From that point on and to this very day I have avoided public criticism of my fellow-writers, no matter how lousy and rotten their crummy efforts may be.

Because of the postdating practices previously mentioned, the January 1935 issue of *Weird Tales* in which I made my bow was actually placed on sale on November 1st, 1934. I would face the remainder of the year — and the entirety of every year yet to come — as a working free-lance author.

My status achieved public attention on my eighteenth birthday, April 5th, 1935. That day a photograph and feature article appeared in the *Milwaukee Journal*'s popular Green Sheet. An interview by a lady journalist disclosed the sort of data no one would come up with until almost half a century later when somebody invented Trivial Pursuits. One of the nuggets in this gold mine of information was the disclosure that I had once spent the night in a cemetery seeking inspiration.

This was not entirely accurate. I had indeed climbed over the wall of Concordia Cemetery one evening during the past summer, but I didn't spend the night there. Nor did I intend to; if so I would have brought my lunch, or at least a midnight snack. As far as I was concerned the cemetery was a nice place to visit but I didn't want to die there.

The newspaper article escalated my ego but not my sales. That year saw the publication of my three subsequent tales, but it wasn't until the end that I began (and continued) selling on a frequent and regular basis. The real benefits of publicity came about a week after the article appeared in the form of an invitation to attend a meeting of the Milwaukee Fictioneers.

As far as I knew, all the members of the Milwaukee Fictioneers were vampires. They only came out at night.

Actually, most of them were moonlighters. Although the term had not yet been invented, the practice was widespread. You had to spread things pretty wide back then if you wanted to make a living as a writer. This was particularly true for those whose writing income, if any, was derived from the pulp magazines.

In faraway New York there were full-time professional writers who sat down to double-martini luncheons with double-dealing editors who reciprocated by giving them story assignments for their magazines. Several scores of these writers ground out wordage at roughly the same rate McDonald's grinds out hamburger meat today. Roughly, but not precisely; the rate for pulp fiction varied from one-tenth of a cent to as much as three cents a word, though a penny a word was generally regarded as the acceptable standard.

But the standard problem was how to make one's work acceptable.

Milwaukee was a far and despairing cry from New York. The number of pulp magazines published there could be counted on the fingers of one sardine. Milwaukee writers had no editors to buy martinis for, or the money to buy them with; a statement which, however ungrammatical, happens to be true.

As a result the city could boast of few published writers. It could, but it didn't. Milwaukee rewarded local authors with a long face and granted them short shrift. Even the latter was hard to come by; during all the years I lived there, the city never gave me any shrift at all. I had to buy my own, which wasn't at all that easy, because I couldn't find out what stores to go to, and I didn't know what the hell a shrift was in the first place.

I didn't know what the Fictioneers were, either, when I received a mysterious phone call inviting me to attend their next meeting. Some kind of literary society, I guessed; maybe there'd be some girls. In any case I had little to lose aside from the carfare which transported me to a duly-designated stop on the near South Side of the city.

Here, stepping out of the shadows to escort me to the meeting site, was a dwarf.

At least that was my first impression of Raymond A. Palmer, an impression quickly dispelled and displaced by the warmth and wit of his personality. Actually he was diminutive rather than dwarfed; a moonlighting science fiction writer who daylighted as a roofer and tinsmith. The evening meeting took place at his family's home.

It was there that I met Ray's fellow-Fictioneers. The all-male unorganized organization had been founded three years previously by its perennial president, Lawrence A. Keating, who specialized in western stories, presumably based upon his own career as a cowboy in La Grange, Illinois. Morry Zenoff and Al Nelson were journalists, which gave them license to write about anything. Larry Sternig was honestly employed, but later turned against humanity by becoming a literary agent. Three members — Leo Schmidt, Bernard Wirth and Dudley Brooks — were university professors, but otherwise decent, law-abiding citizens. Gus Marx and Arthur Tofte churned out fiction on a daily basis as advertising copywriters.

Roger Sherman Hoar was a descendant of Roger Sherman, one of the signers of the Declaration of Independence. Roger himself had been a state senator in Massachusetts, in the Intelligence Service during WWI, made the botanical discovery of the blue dandelion and wrote the first book on constitutional law. As corporation attorney for Bucyrus-Erie, he enjoyed train trips across the country accompanied by a secretary to whom he dictated stories under the pen name of Ralph Milne Farley. A pioneer in science fiction magazines of the Twenties, he was now facing writers who brought new concepts to the field.

One of those younger writers was Stanley G. Weinbaum, who had become a Fictioneer only a year or so previously. In that short span he changed the face of science fiction, without resorting to plastic surgery. Adding badly-needed cosmetic touches of humor, his major operation transformed conventional "bug-eyed monsters" into characters. Usually portrayed as threats, he gave them traits; instead of confining extraterrestrials to actions, he allowed them reactions. All this, mind you, before George Lucas was born.

Taken as a whole, the Milwaukee Fictioneers made quite an impression on me. I learned that they met on Thursday evenings, twice a month, each member playing host in rotation. Coffee and dessert were served, but no alcoholic refreshments. The meetings themselves were informal; reading one's efforts aloud was not allowed. These gatherings were to discuss problems encountered by those who had work in progress, and to help suggest story-ideas for those who did not. It was in many ways the forerunner of today's writers' workshop. Most certainly it was a mutual-aid society; there was never any feeling of competition in the open-floor comments and criticism offered. Despite the disparity in background, education and income-levels there seemed to be a genuine fraternity between these men whose ages ranged from the mature mid-twenties to the elderly mid-forties.

I was later to learn that my rôle at this meeting was that of a prisoner summoned to a hearing before a probation board. Only after passing inspection was a writer free to become a member of the Fictioneers. What sort of discussion took place following my first appearance can only be imagined, but apparently there was no objection to a teen-age weirdo who wrote weirdo stories.

Thus I became a full-fledged member of the Milwaukee Fictioneers at the age of eighteen and so remained for another eighteen years. During that time old members passed on and newcomers, some female, joined the group.

The Fictioneers did a great deal to sustain my feelings of identity at a time and place where writers were regarded — or, more accurately, disregarded — as non-persons. Although only Farley had ever sold a story to *Weird Tales,* I discovered that Weinbaum wanted very much to appear in its pages. We frequently discussed the matter at impromptu interim meetings, during which times he came up with a variety of fascinating story-premises he was never to work on. He died, tragically, a victim of cancer, before the year's end, at the age of thirty-three.

Later I rewrote and sold stories which appeared under the bylines of Ralph Milne Farley and another member, Jim Kjelgaard. But at regular meetings I seldom discussed my own work problems and was never offered a story-premise; matters which didn't disturb me in the least. What the Fictioneers gave me was the opportunity to learn about writing in other fields and find solutions to the problems involved in plotting and characterization.

In due time I collaborated on a play with Lawrence Keating, which we never sold, but it was heartening to be treated as an equal by an older and more experienced writer. Before his death Farley honored me in the Introduction to a collection of his stories, referring to my scientific definitions — "Time is longer than anything." and "Space is just a lot of nothing between stuff." These postulates have yet to be refuted, nor has my gratitude for the help which the Fictioneers gave me.

After joining them I began to take a more professional approach to my own efforts. One of the first things I did was invest several dollars in round-trip trainfare to Chicago, then famed as hog butcher to the world, second largest city in the United States and home of *Weird Tales*. The magazine resided in a fifth-floor, three-room office a few blocks north of the old Chicago Water Tower. One of the inner offices was occupied by editor Farnsworth Wright, the other by managing editor William R. Sprenger. The outer office held a secretary and me, until I was duly summoned to step inside.

Farnsworth Wright was a tall, thin man with a small thin voice. The latter, together with a persistent palsy, was probably due to the effects of Parkinson's disease, an affliction which had plagued him since wartime military service. An authority on Shakespeare and formerly a music critic, this soft-spoken, balding, prematurely-aged man seemed miscast as editor of a publication featuring bimbos uncovered on its covers and horrors concealed within its pages. Bill Sprenger was more boyish and buoyant, but hardly the business manager type. And yet between the two they created a magazine which fulfilled the promise of its masthead — a magazine so truly unique, bizarre, and unusual that its name and reputation survive today.

Thanks to their warm welcome, I survived my first meeting and, during the years that followed, came back for more. Both men had a rare sense of humor, which is probably why they tolerated a teen-age interloper like myself.

It was prior to this meeting that I'd sold them "The Shambler from the Stars," a story in which Lovecraft himself appeared under a pseudonym and a heavy cloud of purple prose. Naturally I had written to Mr. Lovecraft, asking if I could use him as a character and, incidentally, kill him off. He not only agreed but also sent me an official note of permission signed by a number of *his* Cthulhu Mythos characters.

Shortly after my story appeared, one of the readers wrote to the letter-column of the magazine and suggested that Lovecraft might retaliate with a sequel. The notion appealed to him and he promptly set to work on a tale about one Robert Blake, of 620 East Knapp Street, Milwaukee, Wis., who came to Providence and occupied a house which bore more than a passing resemblance to Lovecraft's own. In the end, needless to say, it would have been a lot better for young Mr. Blake if he'd chosen to stay at a Holiday Inn. Luckily for Lovecraft fans, Holiday Inns had not yet been created, or I might not have been destroyed. As it was, "The Haunter of the Dark" saw print in *Weird Tales*. Lovecraft dedicated it to me — the only story of his ever bearing a dedication — and for this I am forever grateful.

Following my Lovecraft *pastiche* it was time to move on. Not yet confident enough to shake off the influence of his style, I could at least explore fresh subject-matter. After a slow start I wrote a yarn dealing with druids, although at that time I had never met one. Then I wrote a story about ghouls, though I had never met one of those either, and didn't until much later, when I went to work in a Hollywood studio. After that I tried a tale with an Egyptian background and subsequently pyramided it into a sequence of stories connected only by common (and all too often, incorrect) mythology. Occasionally there were relapses into Lovecraftean settings but I was gradually undergoing a write of passage.

By now I was becoming somewhat established as a *Weird Tales* contributor and even had a few fans. One of them was a young California resident named Henry Kuttner who worked for his uncle's literary agency but had yet to sell a story of his own. When he did, shortly thereafter, he at once achieved a reputation for himself at *Weird Tales,* a correspondence with Lovecraft, and the basis for a lifetime career. He sent me one of his rejected stories and asked if I'd rewrite it as a collaboration; I did, and "The Black Kiss" was accepted. Years later he suggested his byline be dropped from reprintings because of the degree to which I'd altered the original draft.

Oddly enough, one of my most constant pen-pals was none other than August Derleth, who had only a few years previously offered his critical opinion that I would spend the rest of my life as a nonpublished-person.

Augie, as he was generally known to his fellow-residents in Sauk City, Wis., was eight years my senior and he too had made his first appearance in *Weird Tales* at the age of seventeen. After university graduation he worked briefly as an editor and critic, then became a full-time free-lance short story writer, poet, essayist, dramatist, lecturer, and began a series of historical novels in a regional Wisconsin setting. The first of these had been praised by the then-eminent Sinclair Lewis and thus Augie achieved a stature beyond that of his fellow-writers in *Weird Tales*. He was prodigiously prolific and turned out a book faster than you can say "Stephen King."

On the day I rode the bus to Sauk City for our first meeting, Augie took the day off. He received me at the family home clad in a smoking jacket. This seemed a bit unusual to me, inasmuch as Augie didn't smoke. It did, however, contribute to his image as an Established Author, although in later years he abandoned neckties, long-sleeved shirts and ordinary footwear, even when fulfilling speaking engagements. Burly and barrel-chested, with a booming voice, Derleth was the antithesis of the "artistic type" then envisioned by the general public. He was a man of hearty appetites which he promptly satisfied, as demonstrated when he led me to the local restaurant for lunch and sent the waitress to the corner grocery to buy strawberries for his dessert.

During our meal he expressed hopes of subsidizing a Wisconsin visit for Lovecraft the following summer. Contrary to legend, HPL was not a recluse by choice. In past years I'd received postcards from Quebec, Florida, and New Orleans, but his excursions were limited by economics. Derleth proposed bringing him out to the Midwest where, along with ourselves, he could meet Maurice Moe in Milwaukee and Minnesota resident Donald Wandrei. Naturally he'd also stop by the *Weird Tales* office in Chicago.

"It may turn out after all that the weavers of fantasy are the veritable realists."

Arthur Machen said it long ago, and during the winter of 1936-7 I warmed myself with the thought whenever the rigors of winter weather assailed me.

I hadn't heard very much from Lovecraft after the holiday season, when I may have, as was my usual custom, dispatched him a gaudy crayon-on-cardboard rendering of one of his monsters. I did learn he had seen a physician or intended to see him for a checkup; like myself, he had an aversion to low temperatures. But if he came to Wisconsin during the coming summer, he'd find warm weather and a warm welcome. The thought of meeting him at last was the stuff of fantasy.

Then, on March 15th, Derleth called me from Sauk City to convey the reality. Lovecraft was dead.  Ω

STATEMENT OF OWNERSHIP, MANAGEMENT, AND CIRCULATION
(Required by 39 U.S.C. 3685)

TITLE OF PUBLICATION: *Weird Tales* ®. Publication number: 0985073. Date of filing: 1 October 1990. Frequency of issue: Quarterly. Number of issues published annually: 4. Annual subscription rate: $16.00 [in the United States and its possessions].

Complete mailing address of Known Office of Publication, and of the Headquarters of General Business Offices of the Publisher: both at 4426 Larchwood Ave., Philadelphia [city], Philadelphia [county], PA 19104-3916 (P.O. Box 13418, Philadelphia PA 19101-3418). Full name and complete mailing address of Publisher and Editor: both are George H. Scithers, 4426 Larchwood Ave., Philadelphia PA 19104-3916 (P.O. Box 13418, Philadelphia PA 19101-3418).

Full name and complete mailing address of Managing Editor: Darrell C Schweitzer, 113 Deepdale Rd., Strafford PA 19087. (P.O. Box 13418, Philadelphia PA 19101-3418).

Owner: Terminus Publishing Company, Incorporated, P.O. Box 13418, Philadelphia PA 19101-3418. Names and addresses of *all* stockholders: George H Scithers, 4426 Larchwood Ave., Philadelphia PA 19104-3916. Mary Betancourt, 410 Chester Ave., Moorestown NJ 08057. Leslie Smith, 1209 Miller Ave., Ann Arbor MI 48103. David J Williams III, 5079 Blacksmith Dr., Columbia MD 21044. Darrell Schweitzer, 113 Deepdale Rd., Strafford PA 19087. Yale F Edeiken, 515 Linden St., Allentown PA 18101. There are *no* Bondholders, Mortgagees, or Other Security Holders. This is not a Non-Profit Organization authorized to mail at special rates.

The extent and nature of circulation:

Average number of copies during the preceding 12 months: A. Total number of copies, 12,032. B. Paid and/or requested circulation. (1) Sales through dealers and carriers, street vendors, and counter sales, 4,842. (2) Mail subscription (paid and/or requested), 4,804. C. Total paid and/or requested circulation, 9,646. D. Free distribution by mail carrier or other means, samples, complimentary, and other free copies, 86. Total distribution, 9,732. F. Copies not distributed. (1) Office use, left over, unaccounted, spoiled after printing, 1,968. (2) Returns from news agents, 332. G. Total (sum of E, F (1), and F (2)), 12,032.

Actual number of copies of single issue published nearest to filing date: A. Total number of copies, 12,580. B. Paid and/or requested circulation. (1) Sales through dealers and carriers, street vendors, and counter sales, 4,815. (2) Mail subscription (paid and/or requested), 4,215. C. Total paid and/or requested circulation, 9,030. D. Free distribution by mail carrier or other means, samples, complimentary, and other free copies, 86. Total distribution, 9,116. F. Copies not distributed. (1) Office use, left over, unaccounted, spoiled after printing, 3,187. (2) Returns from news agents, 277. G. Total (sum of E, F (1), and F (2)), 12,580.

I certify that the statements made by me are correct and complete: George H Scithers, Publisher

# TURN, TURN, TURN

## by Nancy Springer

"Well, if that don't take the cake!" Aurie's neighbor lady ogled with gratifying astonishment at the Pringle's Newfangled Potato Chips can Aurie had transformed into an inspiration for all who beheld it. By spray-painting the can glitter gold, cutting an oval in the side and inserting cotton puffs and plastic angels, she had turned it into a portable Heaven complete with snap-fit lid. "My golly days!" the neighbor enthused. "I must say, Aurelia Hess, I have never seen nobody can turn things into something else the way you do." She pointed at the Pringle's can with the posturing fervor of a witness at a murder trial. "You ought to make them things and sell them."

"For the luvva Christ," Aurie's husband, Grant, complained from a nearby armchair, "she don't need to make no more things. The junk we got in this house already is enough to choke a goat."

Both women ignored him: the neighbor, Creda, because she considered him no great bargain, and his wife, Aurelia, because she was contemplating the doily she had glued atop the Pringle's can lid with dissatisfaction. It did not quite cover its plastic matrix as she would have liked. "I should've used a gold sticker on the lid," she said.

"It looks fine just the way it is," Creda chided. "Trouble with you, Aurie, is you ain't never satisfied."

"I'll say," Grant said.

"I just meant in regard to them thingamabobs she makes," Creda told him stiffly. "Hey." She turned back to Aurie. "C'mon over my place, I'll show you what I got."

Aurie went reluctantly, aware that Creda believed they had an interest in common, guiltily knowing it was not so. Creda, taking stolid Pennsylvania Dutch thrift to its logical extreme, was a recycler. She allowed only biodegradable products in her home, and saved her gray water for reuse. She bundled newspapers, collected aluminum scrap and was concerned with tidying up the world. But Aurelia (though she had never said so) did not give a hoot if the whole universe got polluted. Her passion for salvaging Pringle's cans and Dixie Cup spoons frothed from some deep, purely personal font. Some mystic wellspring, hidden in her psyche's wilderness like a Spanish explorer's fountain of gold in a Florida jungle, and she did not herself name or locate or understand it; she knew only that she longed always for — something that blazed like a tropical sun, something more than what she had. Something that was not in her world. Or not yet. Her alchemy was all for herself, for her own life's inchoate goal.

At Creda's place, Aurie admired the new composting john only perfunctorily. Turning plastic soda bottles into porch ornaments engrossed her. Turning this year's shit into next year's vegetables did not.

"I wouldn't want to eat no vegetables been grown in human waste," she told Grant at supper.

Even when he agreed with her he generally found a way to disagree. "Nice talk," he grumbled. "Do we have to talk about it at the supper table?"

She watched him as he downed her best-effort stuffed cabbage. "You like your dinner?" she hinted.

"I'm eating it, ain't I?" In fact, he was eating far too much of it. He was overweight, and wheezed, and though he would not go to the doctor — how many times had she begged him to go to the doctor? — she knew his heart was not good.

"How come you can't say something nice, Grant?"

"How come you're all the time nagging at me? I support you, don't I? I ain't run off with no floozie yet. What the Hell you want?"

It was not a question she could answer.

After she had done the supper dishes and washed the stove, she carried her ineffable yearnings to the spare bedroom where she turned bottles into birdfeeders, six-pack plastics into door wreaths, ham can lids into iron rests, egg cartons into flower arrangements, berry baskets into — she was not sure what she was going to do with the berry baskets. Or the cola caps. Or the turkey neck bones. Or Grant.

The turkey neck bones, boiled clean after Thanksgiving and Christmas, sat pleasantly convoluted to the touch on a pink Styrofoam meat tray, waiting for her to decide what to turn them into. "Would you get rid of them things?" Grant demanded periodically. "They'll draw rats."

"They will not. They're dry." They were, too. Dry and white as her dishpan hands.

Aurie located the grocery bag Creda had just that afternoon given her, a sack filled with tiny plastic cups no bigger than shot glasses. The Methodist Church, it seemed, had started using disposable communion cups when ladies stopped volunteering to wash the glass ones. Creda had told Aurie how she, Creda, had remonstrated with the pastor about this wasteful change, but the best she could do was to get him to rinse and save the plastic ones for her. Now

Creda was counting on Aurie to use the things up.

Aurie sat on the bed and looked at them, reached up to her elbows into the plenitude of them and tumbled them with her hands, feeling her shoulders loosen and her frown soften away as she planned how she was going to turn them into a lamp shield. It would be a lot of work to glue all those little cups together, but no more work than it had been the time she took the innards out of dozens of used flash cubes and turned them into a sparkly picture frame. This lamp shield would be like that, sparkly. Grant wouldn't like it.

She stood up, drifted to the living-room and looked at him.

"You want something?" he asked without shifting his gaze from the TV set.

She said nothing, but stood in the hallway contemplating him and the room. Planters crowded thick on all the windowsills, planters made of any hollow object, of old shoes painted yellow, of those nice margarine tubs with flowers on them, of popsicle sticks log-cabined and lined with those old square freezer containers that the lids never fit right. On the wall was her mosaic made of the good Fiesta Ware dishes she had broken over the years, never being able to bear to throw the bright pieces away. The mosaic portrayed a Mexican boy in a sombrero. Grant didn't like it, or the way she had turned pine cones into little animals for the mantel ("Get them things out of here, they'll draw vermin!"), or the lace-edged plastic-lid coasters on the end tables, or even the ashtrays made out of tuna cans trimmed with black rick-rack to look like truck tires.

The room looked nice, Aurelia decided. Bright. Pretty. But Grant looked out of place in it. He was the only thing in the house she did not seem able to do much with. She had once crocheted sections of beer can (Iron City, his

favorite) together into a baseball hat for him, but he had never worn it.

"What the hun you want standing there, Aurie?"

"Grant," she asked him, "did you ever think of getting a tattoo?"

He looked at her then, bug-eyed. "Great balls of fire, Aurie! What in God's name for?"

"Well, I just thought a tattoo might look nice." Several, actually. She envisioned an angel on his right shoulder, a devil on his left. Flowers and a heart on his chest. Maybe a happy face on his balding forehead, so she'd have something to look at when he had his shirt on.

"If I ever want to throw my money away on that kind of nonsense, I'll let you know."

"Money isn't everything," Aurie said.

"You been sniffing too much of that craft glue of yours." Baffled, Grant gave up on her and turned his attention back to the television.

Later, in the dark of the bedroom, she called softly across the distance between the twin beds, "Grant, do you love me?"

Except for an exasperated sigh, he didn't answer.

"Grant Hess. Do you love me?"

"Holy Gee, woman!" Flat on his back, Grant bellowed straight up at the low ceiling, like a fat calf pinned down for the slaughter. "We been married close to forty years!"

"So?"

"So what the Hell do you think?"

Aurie said, "I'd like to hear you say it once."

"Mush," Grant muttered. "Hogwash." He rolled over with a determined grunt to sleep. His posterior faced her. Cabbage always gave him flatulence. He farted.

Aurie said, "Same to you," got up and padded out barefoot (defiant; he was forever after her to wear her slippers) to look at her balls of string, her sacks of nylon stockings, the gallon milk jugs she

was going to turn into letter holders and vegetable bins and Easter baskets. It was two hours before she came back to bed and went to sleep.

In the morning her husband was dead.

After the first shock of finding him that way (cold and puce-colored), after she had got hold of herself and stopped gulping and shaking, she stood looking at him for a long time. It was her last chance to make anything of him, and before she touched the telephone she needed to think what she wanted to do.

By the time the people came to take him away she had it all quite clear in her mind. "Cremation," she told them.

"There has to be an autopsy."

That did not bother her. No different than taking apart a Raggedy Andy and putting it back together again. And she knew what they would find: a faulty heart. She said, "Right after the autopsy, then, cremate him."

"Are you certain? Have you talked it over with others? Your children? Your pastor?"

There were no children. The pastor was a nincompoop, and so was this pudding-faced undertaker. He just wanted his embalming and casket money, and she knew it. Grant wouldn't have wanted to give him the money either. Though her reasons were different than Grant's would have been. "Cremation," she insisted.

She had thought it out. She knew there were laws against keeping dead relatives around the house in any form except the one she planned. With animals, she understood, it was different. She had once heard of a woman who had had her dead dog freeze-dried and stuffed and had turned it into a foot hassock. But making Grant into a coffee table or anything of that sort was out of the question.

"Cremation," she repeated firmly.

She made appropriate arrangements, conscious but not caring that she had created a small scandal. There were those members of her church who did not approve, but they came to the memorial service anyway, out of curiosity. Some, not sure what to do in the absence of a proper funeral, left offerings of food at the house. Fruit salad. Coffeecake. A Danish ham.

Aurie found herself uninterested in the food, or in taking over Grant's Sunday neckties (which she had long coveted as a source of luxurious fabric for patchwork), or in her sympathy cards, or in much of anything except the large project on which she was working hour after hour while she waited for a package she was expecting.

Several days after the cremation it came: Grant's remains, via registered mail.

She carried the parcel into the house with shaking hands, tore off the brown paper wrapper. In a sturdy plastic box lay an inch of fine ash and a few charred bone chips. Carefully Aurie fished out the chips and put them in the kitchen blender, where she pulverized them to dust. Then with a little water she rinsed the residue into the loaf pan from a Sara Lee Pound Cake. She added the contents of the box, then rinsed it into the pan as well.

She contemplated the box a moment. It was a nice box, far too good to throw out. She would turn it into something. A treasure chest. Maybe decorate it with pasta shells.

It was good to be able to spread newspaper right on the kitchen floor. No need to confine her passion to the spare bedroom now. She had the whole house to herself.

When Creda came over that day (Creda, a good neighbor, had come visiting every day since Grant died), she found Aurelia Hess mixing sparkling gold paint (some kind of texture paint? It had a graininess to it, like it was made with real gold dust) in an aluminum loaf pan that should have been recycled. Creda did not tell Aurie so, of course, not at such a difficult time.

Instead, "Oooh, that's pretty!" Creda encouraged. "What for kind of paint is that? It's nice and thick."

"I gave it some extra body," said Aurie. "For something special I'm working on."

"What's that?"

From the sanctity of the spare bedroom Aurelia brought it out and showed her: a giant creation, wide as her armspread, and she had made it of Swanson's Beef Pie tins and pain, meat trays and cola caps and angry grief, flash cubes and egg-carton flowers and consolation, berry-basket lattice and communion cups and love. And she would paint it gold, gold, gold. Each side of it would be as gold and beautiful as the other. She would string an ornate chain of turkey neck bones painted gold with the thick, shining paint, and she would hang her masterpiece above the armchair, and it would stay there, stirring and shimmering whenever she came near it.

"My stars," Creda said, "Aurie, you sure have got the touch. I've never seen nobody can turn nothing into something the way you can."

Aurie smiled and got down on her knees and started to paint, turning what was left of Grant into a heart of pure gold.

Ω

# THE GRAB BAG

## by Robert Bloch & Henry Kuttner

"I have in this bag," said the little withered man, "a ghost."

No one spoke. They were waiting for the point of the joke. But the little withered man looked almost ludicrously solemn as he continued.

"I do not want this ghost. I wish to sell it. Do I hear ten dollars?"

Somebody handed over a bill. "Thank you," said the little withered man, and went away.

Who he was or how he got in, nobody knew. The week-end party was awash in alcohol and when the host floated his idea of holding an impromptu auction it seemed hilarious. All sorts of fantastic things had been offered for sale — from a used toothbrush to a hen discovered in a neighbor's poultry-coop. Nobody was surprised when Orlin Kyle bought the ghost, for he was the life of the party; a slender chap with cherubic features, much given to gags and practical jokes.

So he bought the ghost, or whatever it might be that the bag really contained. The little withered man had left so hastily and unobtrusively there'd been no opportunity to question him, and it was only later they began to wonder about him and where he'd come from. But nobody wondered much, for the liquor was good, and Kyle was at his facetious best with the bag.

It was a plain burlap sack, bulging but curiously light for all its size. The bulges kept shifting shape, and gave way instantly when squeezed or pressed or prodded through the burlap covering them, so there was no clue as to the bag's actual contents. Its mouth was tightly knotted with thick rope. Kyle slung the sack over one shoulder and wandered around the house, delivering monologues to everybody willing to listen to him. Thanks to intoxication, many thought his infantile attempts at humor amusing — an opinion in which he thoroughly concurred.

Stumbling into the kitchen he found his host, Johnny Vail, blinking at Mrs. Vail over a table clutter of bottles and glasses.

"Here's Orrie," said Mrs. Vail, a tiny, depressed-looking brunette with sad eyes, now slightly glazed.

"And friend," Kyle added. "Can I interest you in a ghost?"

"Have a drink," Vail said.

"That I will. In fact I'll have two."

"Don't be piggy," said Mrs. Vail, reaching for a bottle and a glass.

"I'm not," Kyle told her, sliding a second glass towards the Scotch bottle as she lifted it to pour. "One's for me and one's for the ghost. Spirits for spirits, you know."

"What's all this about ghosts?" Johnny Vail asked.

"That's right — you two didn't wait for the end of the auction, did you?" Kyle explained what had happened, elaborating as he went along. As his story expanded, Vail and his wife began to inspect the bag with maudlin interest.

"And so," Kyle concluded, "I am now the owner of a real live ghost."

"Or a dead cat." Johnny Vail's snigger was both skeptical and unpleasant.

Kyle ignored him, picking up the first glass from the table and downing it at a gulp. As he reached for the second one and raised it to his lips, Mrs. Vail motioned quickly.

"Stop — I thought that was for your ghost."

"Sorry, my mistake. Have to finish it myself. This ghost never drinks on an empty stomach."

Mrs. Vail giggled as she poured herself a generous three fingers, but her eyes strayed to the sack with a nervous quickness. "Orrie, what is in that bag?"

"Let's see." Johnny Vail bent down and lifted the sack gingerly. "Not very heavy, is it?"

"Ghosts don't weigh very much," Kyle said.

Vail ran his right hand along the bulge at the burlap's base. "But there's something inside. Something feels —

*mushy.*"

"Like amorous, you mean?" Fran Vail giggled again. "Give it here, Johnny."

Vail tossed the bag to her. She dropped her glass and it shattered on the floor as she caught the sack. Nobody paid any attention to the mishap.

Fran Vail palpated the side of the sack with a probing forefinger. "You're right, Johnny. I can feel something in here." Her mouth lopsided into a smile and she began to stroke the bulge beneath the cloth. "Nice ghost," she crooned. "Nice —"

Kyle shook his head. "Not at all nice," he whispered. "It's shut up in the bag for a reason. Maybe it has claws. Or teeth."

Johnny Vail snorted. "Then why doesn't it eat its way out of the sack?"

"Doesn't like the taste of burlap," Kyle said, pouring another drink. Glancing up, he gestured. "Wait, Fran — don't stir it up!"

"Why not?" She was fumbling with the rope that bound the mouth. "Stop clowning, Orrie. Le's see what you've really got inside —"

Suddenly Fran Vail broke off with a little shuddering cry and thrust the unopened sack from her. The bag landed soundlessly on the floor and lay there, bulging mysteriously.

"No," she said. "I — I —" Her voice trailed off, but she forced a grin. "Orrie, there *is* something alive in there."

"Sure," Kyle told her. "Dead-alive. Ghost."

Mrs. Vail turned and went to the door. There was a wobble in her walk and a hint of fright in her eyes as she paused in the doorway to glance back at the bag. "Drunker than I thought," she murmured. "Much."

She went into the hall, fingers straying absently about her lips.

Johnny Vail scowled at Kyle. "What the hell's the big idea?" he said. "You scared her. You really scared her."

"Not me." Kyle pointed to the bag. "It."

Vail's fingers fisted. "Look, Orrie, I've had just about enough —"

"Well, have anoth'r and calm down." Kyle picked up the sack and headed for the doorway.

Johnny Vail's voice followed him. "Hey, where you think you're going?"

"After Fran. Got to apologize to her, right?"

"Right." Kyle's host relaxed, waving him on, and he gripped the neck of the sack tightly as he moved along the hall.

He found Mrs. Vail in the parlor, sitting on a couch with two guests. All three had their backs to the hall doorway, but Kyle recognized Fran Vail's companions from an earlier meeting. Pete and Eileen Clement, a young married couple, didn't seem as if they belonged with this crowd. The young man, Kyle remembered, had been one of those polite, look-down-your-nose types. His wife had possibilities, though — a fluffy little thing with big round eyes —

Kyle crept up behind the sofa where they sat and abruptly thrust the bag before Mrs. Vail's startled face. The result surpassed his expectations. She actually looked as though she were going to faint. Jumping up with a cry she pushed the bag aside and moved shakily away. Kyle forestalled her.

Chuckling, he maneuvered the woman into a corner, swinging the sack back and forth for the benefit of the Clements. He noted Pete Clement's eyes narrowing, but Eileen Clement's were widening. Getting her attention was what he wanted. As for Mrs. Vail, he had her attention already, whether he wanted it or not, the stupid cow.

"Don't, Orrie," she said in a strained voice. "Please —"

"Boo! Ghost wants to see you."

"Orrie — I can't —"

"Boo! You wanna see the ghost?"

"No — stop it — please, Orrie —"

"Cut that out," said Pete Clement, getting up from the couch. "It isn't funny!" He was a slim youngster, and

Kyle was encouraged to ignore him until Clement gripped his shoulder and pulled him around.

Kyle dropped the bag and hit Clement in the mouth. The boy staggered back, knocking into Johnny Vail as he entered.

Mrs. Vail seized the opportunity to escape. Kyle started after her, and when Johnny Vail blocked his path, Kyle made the mistake of trying to hit him too.

The result was that Orlin Kyle went over backwards, taking a floor lamp with him, and hit his head hard enough to knock him unconscious.

He woke up to find a blonde girl sitting beside him on the floor. She was holding glasses and a bottle of brandy.

Grunting, he raised himself on one elbow, noting that the dim room was otherwise deserted. Staring at the girl, he rubbed his aching skull.

"Fool," said the blonde. "Here, have a drink. You need it."

The girl was Sandra Owen, Kyle's fiancée. She gave him a glass, poured him a shot, and tilted the bottle to her own lips. They drank together.

"How long've I been out?" he asked.

"Don't know. Someone just told me —"

"Where were you all this time?"

"Around." She forestalled further questioning with a thrust of the bottle. "Have another. Good for the liver."

"Didn't hit me in the liver."

"You should know better than to mess around with Johnny," she said. "He's a creep."

"Wouldn't he go for you?"

Sandra shook her head and pointed to the sack on the floor beside them. "Is that the grab bag I've been hearing so much about?"

"Yeah." Kyle was experimenting with his jaw.

"Where'd you get it."

"Auction." He frowned suddenly. "Damn it, Sandra, where'd you disappear to when it started? I want to know —"

She shook her head. "Answer me first. Who sold you this bag?"

"I don't know. Some old guy, just wandered in. Nobody ever saw him before."

"Fran Vail says you told everyone he was a wizard."

"Just part of the gag."

"Well, she believes it. Claims she's psychic. That's why she's so afraid of what's in the sack."

"Bombed out of her skull, that's what she is," Kyle said. "There's nothing in the sack."

"Have you looked?"

Kyle shook his head. His fingertips were getting numb, so he took another drink.

"Let me see," Sandra said.

"Not yet."

"Why? It doesn't mean anything now. Your gag's a flop."

Or was it? Kyle scowled. He hadn't gone to all this trouble just to get a punch in the jaw. And his gags weren't supposed to end up with the laugh on *him*. There had to be a way to turn the tables. Maybe his fingertips were numb but there was nothing wrong with his brain.

"Look, Sandra," he said. "I have an idea."

Lowering his voice, he told her what had come to him and she listened without comment.

"You'll do it?" Kyle asked.

Sandra nodded. "I've got nothing against *her*, but Johnny is —" She broke off, avoiding his gaze.

Kyle, knowing her, felt suspicion rise in him, but shrugged it away. There was nothing he could do about Sandra's philandering. This girl with the face of a lascivious Mona Lisa was the only thing on earth he loved, and probably the only thing she loved too.

They sat on the floor until they finished the rest of the bottle. By then it was very late and the house was quiet;

the guests had settled down for the night in the upstairs bedrooms.

Kyle and Sandra stumbled up the stairs, then separated to tap discreetly on various doors, whisper to occupants of the rooms behind them. If the taps were sometimes a bit awkward and the whispers a bit slurred, neither of them noticed. They were feeling no pain.

Sandra managed to pull herself together as she lurched down to the end of the hall and knocked on Vail's door. After a while he opened it, rubbing his eyes.

"What is it?" he murmured.

"Orrie. I think he's sick."

"Oh, Orrie." Vail shook his head. "He's just tight."

"No. He's really sick, Johnny. You'll see."

Vail donned a robe and a frown as he followed her down the darkened hallway. The door to her room was ajar and Sandra motioned him in. Then she swiftly pulled the panel shut and locked him in. She moved to a door further along the corridor without waiting to hear Vail's reaction. It was loud and profane, as he realized the trick played upon him.

As Sandra neared the door further down, it opened and Kyle stepped out, the sack dangling from his hand.

"All set?"

"Yeah. Did you lock the Clements in?"

He nodded. "Sure. Now let's get the others out."

It wasn't difficult; not with Johnny Vail pounding on the door at one end of the hall and someone else — probably Pete Clement — hammering away at the other. In a very short time everyone had gathered waiting before the Vails' bedroom, grinning in various stages of intoxication and anticipation. Muffled pounding echoed along the hall behind them.

"Hurry up," Sandra whispered.

Kyle nodded, and opened the door gently. His free hand found the wall

switch. Soft light bathed the room.

Mrs. Vail, bundled under blankets in the twin bed on the far side, had apparently slept through the commotion. Now, startled by the light, she blinked and rolled over on her back.

"The perfect hostess," Sandra said. Behind her, guests were murmuring as they started to crowd into the room. As they watched, Kyle came forward, tiptoeing up to the bedside.

Suddenly he produced the sack from behind his back.

Fran Vail gave a little shriek, but it was drowned in the general laughter.

"We have here," Kyle said, warming to the response of his audience, "a magnif'cent spec'men of ghost. It tells me it wants to see you. Do you want to see it?"

"Orrie," Mrs. Vail whispered. "Stop this, please. Where's Johnny?"

Distant shouting betrayed his whereabouts without any need for Kyle to answer. Instead he swung the bag before her. "Sorry to intrude on your privacy." He gave the word its British pronunciation, which for some reason people tend to find very amusing, particularly if they're hearing it while drunk. "But we talked things over, all of us, and decided the time has come."

"Time? What time?"

"The witching hour. Time to release the ghost."

Kyle's smile and fake accent broadened. "As our hostess, you must do the honors." Suddenly raising the bulging bag, he pushed it forward almost into her face. "Let it out, dear lady," he chuckled. "Let it out."

Fran Vail wasn't chuckling. She began to scream. For a moment her arms flailed in an attempt to brush the sack aside. Then, all at once, she fell back against the pillows and went quite limp. As her eyes rolled upward somebody said, "Cut it out, Orrie. Look what you've done to her."

Others were crowding up to the bed now, remorseful, muttering and chattering as they tried to restore Fran Vail to consciousness. Kyle was pushed aside. He looked around for the sack. Sandra had retrieved it and now she was sitting on the floor in the corner, fumbling with the knotted ropes.

"Hey," he said. "Don't do that."

She stared up at him as though it was difficult for her eyes to find a focus. "Oh, knock it off. You had your fun," she murmured. "Besides, you promised I could if I helped you." Kyle took a step forward and she gestured, eyes slitting. "Get away — don't try t' stop me, hear? Always hogging the limelight — you'n your damn' ghost —" Her fingers scrabbled at the knots. "My turn now —"

Kyle glanced at the group around Mrs. Vail, then hurriedly straightened his shoulders, raised his voice, and called out, "Ladies and gentlemen! Your attention, please!"

Heads turned. Mrs. Vail's eyelids fluttered.

"I present to you the marvel of the age," Kyle said. "Since our hostess is — indisposed — Sandra will now let out the ghost. Invis'ble, impalpable, purch'sed at great expense from a wizard who dared not keep it — I give you the ghost!"

He turned with a wave of his arm, disclosing Sandra as she squatted over the sack. It seemed quite a task, undoing the tangle of knots, and she leaned forward in grim concentration. Quite abruptly the ropes gave way, and as the sack gaped open she lost her balance momentarily, falling forward with a little giggle as her head was enveloped by the burlap folds.

The others echoed ripples of amusement and Kyle laughed too. It was funny, Sandra crouching on her knees with her head tangled in the opening.

But when she swayed and fell sideways it wasn't funny. "Passed out," someone muttered. Kyle bent and pulled the sack free from Sandra's head and shoulders. As he did so he glanced within and saw that it was indeed quite empty. He stood for a moment, looking down into the incredible black emptiness of the grab bag.

Through an alcoholic haze came the cries. His gaze penetrated that same haze, shifting to Sandra. What he saw was a gnawed and tattered crimson horror through which a single glazed eye stared up blindly. Something had eaten Sandra's face.

Ω

# FISHER DEATH

Stricken by favors of a darkened place
Falling through limbo
    upon fractured wings
Greeted in deserts by scorpion stings
Glaring at Love without eyes in its face.
Sifting through dust
    that was once a great God
Laughing in echoes
    that fade without trace
Twined in our graveclothes
    of gossamer lace

Peering in chasms
    where light is outlawed.

Tears fall like knives into the fearful pit,
Spirits glint like moonbows in jet cascade
Sought by Fisher Death
    for his waiting spit.
Fear not. Even this indignity will fade.
Trampled beneath our impossible dreams,
Vanished in rips in reality's seams.

**— Jessica Amanda Salmonson**

# MOTHRASAURUS

## I

They watch her.
(From under beds, tops of pillows, silky surfaces of china mugs, they watch her)
Elongated necks, ridge of bone, walnut-small brains, backing the tiny eyes that flatly observe
    (coiling, buried, the old thoughts of green
    and steaming earth and air, now overlaid
    with dusty nap of rug, mists of Glade and
    Arm and Hammer)
the woman; watch her bend and crawl after them, grabbing and placing them among their fellow watchers . . .
. . . on the shelves and in the toyboxes of her running young.

## II

She cannot escape them.
(Puzzles on the floor, flash-cards in the children's hands, resting under lunch plates and silverware, hiding in oval soap)
Day-glo colors, plush fur skin, pencil-sharpener mouths, "Three-horned face" logo on her children's shirts
    (they inundate their letters to Santa, their
    rubbery bodies line the bathtub floor, and
    still they come, invading cereal box covers)
all dinosaurs; see the children follow their outlines in cut-paper stencils, color them in with Brontosaurus-yellow markers . . .
. . . while the Stegosaurus and Protoceratops eye the Mother.

## III

Ankylosaurus, Allosaurus
    (once, the living rooms and dinettes were their jungles,
their places of green leaves and water for sucking, swallowing)
    Tyrannosaurus, Triceratops
    (yesterday, they pounded the earth with their large steps,
and the air around them was clear-pure and green-smelling)
    Pterosaurus, Pterodactyl
    (not so very long ago, they ruled, a minute ago in the cosmic
clock of hours . . . and for the old, a minute is short)

## IV

Partyware, Placemats
    (only a year ago the children clamored for vegetable name
dolls and remote-control cars they saw dance and spin on the idiot box)
    Tee-shirts, Tape measures

(then came the first of them, innocent enough, *something to*
teach them, she thought, *something of the past that* interests *them*)
Corkboards, Coloring books
   (until the day came when the children's every other word ended
in "saurus" and they played brutal dinosaur games, as they roared)

## V

Their time is returning.
(In every home of every child, they sit, becoming part of the fiber
of their existence, filtering into consciousness)
   They attend the meals, bob about in the bathwater, support pieces
of birthday cake, come to life with the joining of jigsaw fragments
         (today immobile, too strange to move yet,
         yet with repeated familiarity comes freedom,
         acceptance . . . from the running young)
   bearing their imprint; with the remembering of their past comes
new life, new chances for dominance . . .
. . . in the world of the cornered woman.

## VI

She has realized their plan.
(The Old Ones will return, or so Lovecraft hinted, speaking of things
big, huge and malevolent, things that *wait*)
   their names twist and writhe, Protoceratops and Dimetrodon, yet
flow smoothly off the tongues of the young
         (the children worship them, pay lip service
         with each opening of the cereal box, each turn
         of the dinosaur skeleton's key . . . and she's
         seen their eyes shift)
   dinosaur slaves; the children clamor for the ancients, ignore
the new and living to immerse themselves in the bony dead . . .
. . . who watch the woman with baleful flat-paint eyes.

## VII

December the eighth started out as a normal day
         (fix breakfast, pack lunches in
         Brontosaurus bags, cover little
         Triceratops tee-shirts with coats,
         mufflers)
until the mother found the puddle of wetness on the
children's sheets . . . the pool of moistness, green and scummy
   with the live Trilobite crawling on the wet polyester —
         ("terrible lizard," that's what the
         children said the word "dinosaur"
         meant)
— next to the single shed scale.

**— A. R. Morlan**

# WEIRD TALES TALKS AGAIN WITH ROBERT BLOCH

## by Bradley H. Sinor

**Weird Tales:** The majority of your writing has been concerning the darker side of human nature. Why is this?

**Bloch:** Curiosity. I've never been able to understand the fascination and delight that some people take in inflicting pain, be it real or emotional, injuring or killing other people or animals. That's why a lot of my stories are written from the point of view of the psychopaths; it helps me understand them better.

**WT:** What do you think goes into making up a good horror story?

**Bloch:** Fear is the main thing. Only it has to be a fear that is close to reality, something that people can recognize as part of the world around them. The more familiar, the stronger it is.

If you use something that is different, it has to fit into the inner story-logic and rationale that you've established. The closer you can get to reality, the better off you are.

Lovecraft was a prime example. He took the discovery of Pluto, of a new planet in mankind's universe, and built a part of his mythos from it. That's what he used as a basis to build fear on.

It's instinctive for people to be afraid of the dark, pain, or the possibility of death or injury. In today's society that can include the violence on the streets.

After that it is all a matter of the writer's technique and style.

**WT:** Do you have any particular writing techniques you use when you're working?

**Bloch:** I generally have an ending in mind. Then I try to do some sort of a short synopsis. I like to know where it is that I'm going when I tell a story and how I'm going to get there. I certainly wouldn't think of taking a trip without a map or a destination in mind. If it's a novel rather than short fiction that just means that there are more byways and interchanges to explore.

**WT:** One of your novels is called *Lori,* isn't it?

**Bloch:** Right.

**WT:** How would you describe it?

**Bloch:** *Lori* started out as a charming little story about a young girl and her teddy bear. Somewhere along the line we lost the teddy bear, the girl grew up, and people started trying to kill her.

**WT:** I understand that the publisher is marketing it as horror.

**Bloch:** That's what I've been told. I'd call it a mystery suspense story with elements of both science fiction and fantasy.

**WT:** As I understand it, H.P. Lovecraft was the one who got you started as a writer.

**Bloch:** It certainly was. There wouldn't have been a first story if it hadn't been for Lovecraft.

In excerpts from my recently written autobiography I've detailed how teen-age correspondence with Lovecraft encouraged me to attempt writing fantasy and supernatural stories for *Weird Tales.*

**WT:** What about science fiction?

**Bloch:** That came later. So did the humorous efforts — at least those I consciously intended to be humorous. Some of the serious stories were pretty funny, but I didn't know it at the time.

**WT:** When did you become an advertising copywriter?

**Bloch:** Shortly after I discovered that a wife and child require daily supplies of food on a year-round basis.

**WT:** But you continued to write fiction on the side?

**Bloch:** And on the job. During my years of incarceration at the advertising agency I wrote well over a hundred stories and a radio series, *Stay Tuned for Terror.* Many of the thirty-nine shows I scripted were adapted from yarns I'd written for *Weird Tales*. The magazine generously advertised and promoted this program, which was terminated abruptly at the end of the first season when the producer died in the tragic crash of his private plane.

**WT:** So you went back to writing for print?

**Bloch:** I'd never had sense enough to stop. Before leaving advertising in 1953 to resume a full-time career of starvation, I'd sold my first two mystery-suspense novels, *The Scarf* and *Spiderweb*. Over the next five years I wrote articles, columns, another hundred or so short stories and novelettes, plus three more novels. Way back in 1948 I'd been guest of honor at the World Science Fiction Convention in Toronto, and a decade later, won a Hugo Award for a short story. Now, as 1959 loomed, I'd already logged a quarter century as an active professional writer. But about the only effort I was usually identified with was a little opus titled "Yours Truly, Jack the Ripper," which had first appeared in *Weird Tales* for July, 1943.

**WT:** Then came *Psycho*.

**Bloch:** And still keeps coming even today, I'm afraid.

**WT:** Do you ever get tired of having people ask about *Psycho* rather than your other work?

**Bloch:** Not tired, just used to it. After a certain point you have to develop a certain amount of scar tissue, otherwise you're going to bleed to death. Actually,

if you've got some questions about *Psycho,* go right ahead and ask them, I don't mind.

**WT:** Okay. The popular belief is that you based *Psycho* on an actual killer. Is this true?

**Bloch:** No, it isn't. The case they're talking about is the Ed Gein case in Wisconsin. I based *Psycho* on that situation rather than on Gein. I read accounts of the case in the newspaper and the whole idea fascinated me; that someone living in a small town could indulge in what we've come to call serial killings without any of his neighbors being any the wiser.

I sat down and tried to figure out how this could happen. The result was a novel that I called *Psycho*. Years later I discovered that my completely imaginary Norman Bates and the accused killer actually had a lot in common. But I didn't use Gein as a model.

**WT:** When you sold the movie rights on *Psycho* you didn't have any idea that it was Hitchcock who was buying them?

**Bloch:** That's right. It was what was called a blind buy. I think if they'd had their eyes open they would have passed on it. MCA refused to tell either my agent or me who it was. I think it was to keep us from raising the price.

**WT:** Did you ever actually meet with Hitchcock?

**Bloch:** Yes, but not until after the filming was completed. By that time I was living on the West Coast. Hitchcock knew and invited me to a screening of the rough-cut. He sat behind me, along with Janet Leigh and Bernard Herrman, the composer.

After it was over, he introduced himself and asked "What do you think?" I told him, "Sir, this will either be your greatest success or the biggest bomb you ever made!"

**WT:** What did you think of the sequels?

**Bloch:** Haven't seen either one of them, although I did see copies of the scripts. Most of what I hear about any sequels is strictly hearsay. Like the reports of a *Psycho IV* being made. The only thing that I know about it is that someone had seen a mention of it in the newspaper.

**WT:** Any particular reason you didn't see them?

**Bloch:** Because I'm really rather squeamish by nature, when it comes to excessive violence. Since I don't commit it myself on paper I don't particularly care to see it done by others on the screen.

**WT:** You wrote your own sequel to your original novel, fittingly called *Psycho II*, which had nothing at all to do with the movies. Has there been any sort of film interest in the novel?

**Bloch:** Not that I know of. But it wouldn't do any good. When my agent sold the theatrical rights to the first book it included all rights to the *Psycho* concept in perpetuity. So I get nothing from any of the sequels, be it *Psycho II, III, IV, XVIII, LVI,* or whatever. I also get nothing from any t-shirts, postcards, shower curtains or any of the other merchandising.

**WT:** They tried to spin a television series off from the movies, didn't they?

**Bloch:** That's what I understand. I think it was called *The Bates Motel.* I didn't see that one either. When I heard about the idea I thought it was foredoomed and it was.

**WT:** Did your initial move to the West Coast to write for television and feature films have anything to do with the movie version of *Psycho*?

**Bloch:** No, my move had nothing to do with the film. It was still being shot when I first came out to California in October, 1959. A writer friend of mine had gotten me an invitation to write an episode of a syndicated show called *Lockup*.

The whole idea was presented to me as a no-lose proposition. My friend told the show's producer that if they didn't

like the script I turned in, he would write one in its place.

The worst that I would get out of the deal was what amounted to a three-week paid vacation. I'd done radio scripts for years but I didn't know if I could really write for television; this seemed like a good way to find out.

**WT:** You'd already worked extensively in radio. Did you do anything special for your first venture into television scripting?

**Bloch:** I didn't look at any of my friend's scripts, or at anyone else's for that matter. I had an idea of the sort of story that I wanted to write. So I got one script from the show itself, mainly to act as a guideline. The producers liked what they saw and asked for another and another. I ended up doing six in all.

**WT:** You mentioned that something odd had recently happened to you as a result of your earlier television writing.

**Bloch:** [Laughs] Yes, indeed. Back in 1959 one of the first scripts that I wrote for the *Lockup* series starred a young actor by the name of Macdonald Carey. He also ended up starring in one of the first *Thriller* scripts that I did. We never met at the time and in the ensuing years our paths never crossed.

Then just a week ago [July 1989], I was at an autographing for *Lori* over in Brentwood. Here I am minding my own business and this man walks up and sits down next to me and says, "Hello, my name is Macdonald Carey."

He had heard that I was going to be there and wanted to meet me. I was really quite flattered that he had taken the trouble. Since I don't watch the daytime soaps I really had no idea what he'd been doing all these years. [Carey has starred for over twenty years on the daily soap opera *Days of Our Lives*.] He's a poet as well and gave me a copy of his third book of published poetry.

**WT:** If I recall correctly you did three scripts for the original *Star Trek* television series: "What Are Little Girls Made

Of ?", "Catspaw," and "A Wolf in the Fold."

**Bloch:** That's correct.

**WT:** Did the producers of *Star Trek: The Next Generation* approach you about writing for the series?

**Bloch:** They certainly did. So far as I know I was the only writer who had worked on the original series that they invited back. I would have really liked to have done something for them, if just for sentimental reasons.

Unfortunately, I had to turn them down. I was behind on finishing some novels that I was committed to doing and just didn't have the necessary time.

**WT:** In the years since you broke in, how has writing for television changed?

**Bloch:** It's a lot more difficult now. There was a time when you went in to see a producer or a story editor. They either liked what you suggested, offered you a story that they wanted adapted, or suggested one of your own that might fit.

Today you don't have anything like that situation. The surface may look the same, but there have been some major changes. With conglomerates and mergers, quite often the outfit you're writing for isn't owned by who you think it is. So instead of writing for one person you are writing for this vast committee, the majority of which are in New York while you're out in California. A judge and jury decide the fate of your work and you never see them nor they you.

**WT:** About the movies that you've scripted: have you liked what finally reached the screen?

**Bloch:** A little bit. There was around 20 minutes of *Straitjacket* that I was pleased with. Along with the first segment of *Asylum*. They shot them exactly the way that I wrote them, which doesn't happen too often.

**WT:** What projects are you currently working on?

**Bloch:** I'm editing a two-volume anthology of horror stories, with the help of Martin H. Greenberg. The working title is *Psycho Paths*.

I have also collaborated on a fantasy novel with Andre Norton. Its title is *The Jekyll Legacy,* and it's a sequel to Stevenson's famous work. Tor is our publisher. That project came about after I contributed a short story to one of her *Witch World* collections.

Tor also publishes my next novel, *Psycho House.* I'll leave it to you to guess what that one's about.

**WT:** Thank you for your time, Mr. Bloch.

**Bloch:** You're quite welcome.

Ω

# OTHERWHERE

**O** bscure images flicker on the air,
**T** hreadlike glimpses no other eye can share.
**H** ints of some world, uniquely strange and rare,
**E** xplode brightly then vanish as I stare.
**R** ivers oddly purple, yet cool and fair,
**W** rest me from the city's hot summer glare.
**H** umdrum though the days which stretch bleak and bare,
**E** lysian sights relieve my dark despair.
**R** eason may call me mad, yet I know there
**E** xists a world which waits for me . . . otherwhere.

— **Walter Shedlofsky**

# PLAYING FOR KEEPS

## by Lawrence Watt-Evans

Carefully, Jason leaned out the open window and peered about. The moon was half full, providing him with plenty of light to see that the side lawn was smooth and empty, the hedge dark and unbroken. Nothing moved, nothing was out of place.

He pulled his head back in and listened for a moment. He heard nothing but crickets and his own breathing; his parents and his kid sister were, he was sure, sound asleep.

The coast was clear.

Cautiously, he climbed headfirst out the window onto the porch roof, then pulled himself down the sloping asphalt shingles on his belly. At the edge he reached down and grasped the corner pillar, then gradually worked his feet around, crab-fashion, until he was able to swing his left leg down onto a foothold in the gingerbread.

From there it was easy; he slid the other leg around and shinnied quickly down the pole to the railing, and dropped from there down behind the bushes.

The bushes rustled more than he liked, and he froze for a moment, staring out at the vacant lawn gleaming silver in the moonlight.

The way was still clear. He was out of the house, free to roam. He could slip down to the pond and catch himself a frog without his parents knowing a thing about it.

He gazed critically at the wide back yard, and decided that it was too open, too visible. He would find another route, rather than cutting straight across all that lawn.

The hedge that ran along the boundary with the MacPhersons' yard would provide cover. He could follow it to the back corner, then make a short dash to the trees, and from there to the pond it was all woods.

A dash across the side yard, the long creep down the hedge, another dash, and the woods. It would be easy. It would be fun, too, as if he were a soldier dodging bullets or something. He crept out from behind the bush, looked quickly to either side, and ran.

A dozen steps and he was across the lawn, diving for the shelter of the hedge's shadow. He landed on his knees and elbows with his nose inches from the leaves, leaves that looked dead black in the pale light.

He glanced back at the lawn just in time to see the shadow stretch out across the grass.

Horrified, he looked up.

A figure loomed over him, shadowy black, tall, taller than seemed possible, its head bloated and misshapen. He gaped up in surprise. He fought down the urge to cry or scream as a gaunt hand reached down toward him.

The hand grabbed him by the back of his collar and hauled him upright, then yanked him clean off his feet. He dangled helplessly.

"Guess what, kid," a deep, deep voice said, "I'm the boogey man."

He wanted to say something smart, something scathing, in reply to this terrifying stranger, but all he could manage was, "No, you're not; there isn't any boogey man."

Teeth glinted as his captor smiled. "Maybe you're right, boy; maybe I'm not. But I might as well be. Now, you must be Jason Price; why don't we go see what your parents think about you being out at this hour?" He casually lifted the struggling boy over the hedge and marched up toward the street, Jason still dangling from his hand.

From his altered angle Jason could see his foe more clearly; he was no longer a mass of empty shadow. The weird bloating of the head was really just a battered, wide-brimmed felt hat; the teeth were flat, human teeth, the eyes dark and smiling, the hands large, but just hands, with only five fingers apiece. He was just a man, whoever he was.

They reached the street and turned left, toward Jason's house, and Jason demanded, "Put me down; I'll walk from here."

"I don't think so," the other replied; he marched on.

"You're ruining my shirt," Jason complained.

His captor shrugged. "That's too bad."

He turned and marched up the front walk, strode smoothly up the porch steps, and with the boy still dangling from his right hand, rang the bell with his left.

There was a long moment's wait, and Jason heard banging and voices within. The porch light flashed on and his father opened the door, wearing his old bathrobe.

"What is it?" he asked, blinking.

"Mr. Price?" the self-proclaimed boogey man said, "I believe this belongs to you." He held Jason up to the light.

"Jason?" Price gaped, then remembered himself. "Oh, of course. Thank you, Mr. Crowley. Where'd you catch him?"

"Oh, I happened to be behind the hedge next door when he climbed down the porch."

"Oh. Well, thank you; put him down, I'll take care of him now."

"All right." Crowley lowered Jason roughly, not quite dropping him. "He's all yours for now, Mr. Price."

"Thank you, Mr. Crowley."

"Just remember," Crowley said with a broad smile, "The third time I keep him."

Price managed a feeble reflection of the other's grin. "Of course." He grabbed Jason's arm and hauled him into the house. "Good night, Mr. Crowley; thanks again."

Crowley tipped his hat and stood, smiling, as Price closed the door.

As soon as the latch clicked into place, Jason demanded, "Who's that guy? What was he doin' back there?"

"Never mind who that is, Jason; what the Hell were you doing outside at this hour?"

"Aw, Jesus, Dad, I just wanted to go down to the pond and catch some frogs when there wasn't anybody else around to scare 'em off!"

"Well, you'll have to find some better time to do it than the middle of the night! Don't you know it's dangerous running around in the dark? You could get arrested, or attacked. You're lucky it was Mr. Crowley who found you, and not some pervert!"

"How do you know *Crowley's* not a pervert?" Jason countered.

"Well, if you must know, he's the new security patrolman for the block; the Neighborhood Council hired him last month."

"So what business is it of his if I go catch frogs?"

"That's one of the things we're paying him for, to make sure you kids don't go running around at all hours, so we don't have teenagers screwing in the woods back there."

"What's that got to do with me? I'm only eleven!"

"And that's too damn young to be running around at two in the morning!" Price bellowed.

Jason sensed that he wasn't going to get anywhere by arguing his right to roam free at night. "I still think Crowley's a pervert!" he said, trying a different tack.

"We checked him out, boy, don't you think we didn't — and if he *is* a pervert, that's all the more reason for you to stay in at night the way you're supposed to, so he won't catch you again!"

Jason couldn't think of an answer to that; he shut up and stared at his father in silent defiance.

He wasn't actually punished, just sent back to bed. He watched his father close and lock the window, then stamp out and close the door. He sat in bed, thinking, and it was a long hour before he finally slid down and fell asleep.

The following night he stayed inside, but spent two hours crouched at the window, watching the yard, watching the MacPhersons' yard, studying every detail of the hedge in between, leaning over to stare at the woods far off to the right.

He saw no sign of Crowley, but he didn't risk climbing out; he had seen no sign of Crowley before he was caught, either.

The next day, at school, one of the kids mentioned "the boogey man," and Jason was surprised to hear that half a dozen of his friends knew about Crowley's presence. In fact, some knew considerably more than he did.

"He's six foot five, my dad says," Bill Jenkins told him, "Six foot five, and he weighs a hunnerd and sixty-five pounds, but he's strong enough to pick a kid up and carry him like he weighs nuthin'."

Jason nodded agreement. "He's strong, all right."

"He lives in the top floor apartment at that place on Elm, the one with that tower on the corner, and he sleeps all day and only comes out at night. He was like that anyway, that's why they hired him."

"Maybe there's something wrong with him, so he can't stand the sun," Sam Hessen suggested.

"Maybe he's really the boogey man, like he says," Jim Fairleigh said.

"There ain't any boogey man!" Jason said.

"How d'you know?" Jim countered.

"There just ain't," Jason insisted. "He's like Santa Claus or the Easter Bunny, something the grown-ups use to get kids to behave."

"Well, this Crowley guy sure is strange, whether he's the boogey man or not," Bill said. "He *tells* everybody he's the boogey man."

"I think he's a pervert," Jason said.

"Naw," Bill said, "They wouldn't hire a perv!"

"How would they know?"

"Well, he ain't never been arrested, I heard my dad tell my mom that. Clean record, he says."

"If he's really the boogey man they wouldn't have caught him," Jim pointed out.

"There ain't any boogey man," Jason insisted.

"Where'd they find him?" Sam asked.

"*I* don't know," Bill replied. Nobody else volunteered any more information.

Jason mulled it all over, and after he had given it sufficient thought, he announced to his friends, "I'm not gonna take it."

"What aren't you gonna take?" Sam asked.

"I'm not gonna take this Crowley character or any of his boogey man crap. It's a free country, ain't it? Who's he to tell me I can't take a walk in the middle of the night if I want?"

"He's just doin' what our parents want, that's all," Joe Kimball said. "I don't think it's his idea. I kinda think he likes kids, from what I seen; he's always makin' jokes and smilin', talkin' about how he'd like to keep 'em."

"Well, I'm not gonna take it," Jason insisted.

"Suit yourself," Bill said with a shrug, "But *I'm* not gonna argue with him."

The bell rang, putting an end to the

conversation.

That night Jason watched out his window again, very carefully, starting the moment his bedroom door was closed. He saw no sign of Crowley anywhere. He waited and watched.

The moon was two-thirds full, the sky was clear, and Jason saw no sign of Crowley. He heard the crickets chirping, an occasional frog calling faintly to him from the pond.

Finally, at half past two, he slid out the window onto the porch roof and made his way to the ground.

From the bushes by the porch he stared critically at the hedge. That had been his mistake, he decided, going to the hedge. Crowley might be lurking there right now, and even if he weren't he could sneak along the other side and Jason wouldn't be able to spot him.

If he were to go straight across the back lawn, though, Crowley wouldn't have anywhere to hide, and Jason didn't think he was the sort who would chase a kid halfway across town. No, Jason told himself, Crowley was an ambusher; it went with the calm smiling style.

With that in mind, he slipped out from behind the bushes and headed straight back toward the trees, across the open expanse of lawn.

As he passed the back corner of the house something grabbed the back of his shirt, and he was snatched up into the air.

"Guess what, Jason," that deep voice said, "It's the boogey man, and I've got you again."

Jason was furious; how could he have been caught so easily? He thrashed, kicking, and tried to drive his elbow back into Crowley's chest.

Crowley did not bother with subtlety; his left hand flashed out as his right twisted, and his long bony fingers clamped around Jason's throat.

"Stop it, boy," he said.

Jason struggled for another few seconds, then stopped as his air supply ran out. The grip loosened.

"Listen to me, Jason," Crowley said, "I don't want any of this from you. I caught you where you had no business being, outside at this hour; now you behave yourself, or you'll get a lot worse than anything you've got from me yet."

The voice was flat and deadly, and Jason believed it completely. He put up no further resistance as the rest of the scene was acted out much as before. He was carried helplessly to his front porch, the doorbell brought his father, and Price and Crowley exchanged polite words, Crowley smiling all the time. He was then left in his father's custody.

This time he didn't talk back or argue; the memory of that grip on his throat was too fresh. He nodded quietly and went back to bed when his father had finished yelling.

The next day, however, the pain and fright had faded, and his indignation had begun to mount. How had Crowley dared to treat him like that? He was an innocent child, not some kind of axe-murderer trying to escape. His parents were paying their fake boogey man to protect them, not to manhandle their children. What if his larynx had collapsed? He'd seen that happen on a doctor show on TV, and the person had almost died, and they had had to cut her throat open and stick tubes in.

He told himself that he should have complained, should have said something to his father. Why hadn't he?

Well, he decided, it wasn't Dad's business; this was between him and Crowley. He'd handle it on his own. He was almost twelve now, old enough to take care of himself.

Besides, he wasn't sure that his father would believe him. A glance in the mirror showed no bruises or other marks on his neck.

He thought about it for the rest of the day, making plans, and that afternoon, while he was at Sam's house and Sam was in the bathroom, he snuck into

Sam's older brother Al's room. He knew that Al had what he wanted; he'd seen him show it off once, and had seen where he put it afterward.

It was right where he had seen it before. He stuck it in his pocket and hurried back out of the room before he was caught.

That night it rained, and Jason stayed inside. He woke up briefly around three and glanced out the window, and thought he saw something tall and dark moving across the lawn. Before he could focus on it it was gone; he stared futilely for a few minutes, then went back to bed.

The rain lingered through the following day and night, but the day after that was sunny and warm, a lovely spring day.

Night arrived, and Jason watched television disinterestedly as he pretended to do his math homework. Finally, at ten-thirty, his mother turned off the set and shooed him upstairs.

He lay awake in bed waiting.

At one, he rose and dressed silently, then fished his stolen prize from its hiding place in his bureau drawer. With it safe in his pocket he crossed to the window and opened it.

The night air was cool and fresh, the singing of the crickets soothing, but Jason wasn't concerned with that. He stared out at the lawn, studied every foot of the hedge, peered at the back corner of the house.

He didn't see Crowley, but he had no doubt that the tall dark man was out there, waiting.

He hoped he was out there. He intended to show this Mr. Crowley that Jason Price wasn't just a rag doll you could throw around as you pleased.

He climbed out onto the porch roof, made his way to the ground, and without preamble marched boldly out across the lawn.

Crowley reared up from behind the hedge, his shadow falling across Jason

so suddenly that the boy started. Jason's hand dove into his pocket.

Crowley stepped through the hedge with a hissing of branches against cloth, and strode purposefully toward Jason.

"Not this time, Mr. Boogey Man!" Jason said as he whipped out the switchblade and pressed the button.

Crowley didn't say a word; he just kept coming, one slow deliberate step at a time.

That wasn't in the plan; Jason had thought that Crowley would stop at the sight of the knife shining silver in the moonlight, would stand back frightened, and Jason had planned out a little speech, telling him that he couldn't bully Jason Price. But Crowley wasn't stopping.

He finally came to a halt one step away from Jason, staring down at the boy from the black shadows of his decrepit hat.

"Get away from me!" Jason said, brandishing the knife.

Crowley reached out with both hands, reached out and hooked his fingers into the front of Jason's shirt. He hooked his fingers into the fabric and clenched them into fists, and started to pick Jason up off the ground.

"No!" Jason shouted; he stabbed wildly.

Crowley gave a little grunt as the knife was jammed into his belly, and the world froze for the two of them.

Jason stared in utter horror at his hand, at the short little slit he had cut in Crowley's flannel shirt, and at the gleaming steel blade that joined the two, the blade that was sunk three inches into Crowley's flesh.

He hadn't meant for this to happen. He had just committed murder. He had stabbed a human being, stuck a knife into a man.

All he had wanted to do was scare the man, the way the man had scared him. He hadn't meant to hurt anyone. He was a good boy, not a trouble-maker or a delinquent.

He was going to jail, and the other prisoners, the *real* murderers, would beat him and do whatever the terrible things were that men did to each other, and he might be stabbed himself, might feel the steel biting into him and his blood spilling out hot and red. He stared in fascinated revulsion at the knife, at the gleaming steel blade embedded in Mr. Crowley's belly.

He realized, at last, that the blade was clean. There was no blood.

The hands tightened on his shirt and yanked upward, and the moment of frozen time was broken and gone. The knife pulled out of the flesh, and still no blood flowed. Instead Jason smelled burning, hot and metallic, and saw a wisp of black smoke curling up. The tip of the switchblade was black where it had gone in.

His eyes moved up across Crowley's chest to his face, a face that was somehow changed from what it had been, as if a mask had come off. The tall figure grinned, and a dusky red glow showed between jagged teeth. His eyes gleamed dark green around slit pupils.

"Guess what, Jason," that deep and terrible voice said. "I really *am* the boogey man." The grin widened, the red glow brightened.

"And the third time, I keep you."    Ω

## THE SORCERER IN HIS WRATH

### 1

Now is the time for the breaking of graves,
for the hour of vengeance has come 'round at last.
Now shall the dead lie embracing the living —
Let their foul kisses bring sharp screams of love!

I stand here in darkness while tall cities tumble,
while gold-drapèd corpses usurp the world's thrones.
I speak words of fire, of tempest, of earthquake:
My orison horror, and death my Amen.

### 2

Yet would I ask in a quieter voice,
what fool is this man who would thunder the skies?
What arrogant ass who thinks that his rage
should speed on its way the mere passage of years?

This surely is Time's work: the ravening scythe,
the merciless glass, the withering touch.
When this one like all men is pitiful dust,
what matter his anger, his vengeance, his name?

— **Darrell Schweitzer**

# RUMORS

# OF

# GREATNESS

by
Nina
Kiriki
Hoffman

Regina set Leroy on his blanket where he could look at the Christmas tree. Its lights twinkled, tiny soundless bursts of color that bounced reflections off the shining ornaments and cast the pine needles in silhouette. The house bore the scent of pine like an incense fog.

Kneeling beside her son, Regina watched his eyes as reflected light danced across them. She could see his delight. He waved his fists and gurgled with pleasure.

"Yes, little one, beautiful, all for you," she said. She smiled, thinking about the cup of tea she had drunk the day before the baby was born. She had sipped it, and when she finished, the tea leaves lay in a ragged circle at the bottom of the cup, a crown, or perhaps a ring. Destined for greatness. The tea leaves were only the last link in a chain of omens she had received since she learned she was pregnant.

"Lullay, thou little tiny child," she sang, remembering the tall stranger she had passed in the street when her belly was just starting to globe. Buildings baked in the first onslaught of summer sun. City traffic whizzed by, leaving fumes behind. The quart of milk she carried was sweating in her hands. The stranger, one of a flow of people passing her, stopped and stared at her. He had hair like ice and eyes like fire. He laid one pale, long-fingered hand on her belly and said to her, "Blessed art thou among women, and blessed be the fruit of thy womb. The Lord is with you."

She had felt radiant energy in his touch. It shone through her as if she were glass, and the babe within her moved beneath the stranger's hand.

"Bye, bye, lully, lullay."

Leroy turned from his contemplation of the tree and looked up into her face. The crown jewel — she called it that, anyway; it was a gold pendant with a green stone inset that someone had given her while she was recuperating after Leroy's birth at the hospital — lay on the white of his shirt, its stone hosting flashes of light in echo of the lights on the tree.

"Lullay, thou little tiny child," she sang. His face had gone sober. As much as she loved his smiles, she loved his wide-eyed wondering looks even more.

"Bye, bye, lully, lullay."

The last notes hung in the air like snowflakes, then melted. Leroy's slow smile surfaced. He reached up a hand, and she leaned down, putting her face in range. He touched her lips. She felt the same strange tingle from his fingertips she had felt when the stranger touched her. "Oh, my little one, who will you be when you grow up? Will you save the nations? Will you spread peace, scatter it across the world like seeds? Will you work out of a throne room or an oval office or a pulpit?"

Leroy tapped her lips as she spoke. His smile widened.

For a moment his face filled her thoughts, his wonderful, honey-gold face with its high forehead, large, long-lashed black eyes, smiling mouth. His black hair was curly. She felt an adoration so strong it was an ache.

She glanced toward the tree, her eyes sheathed in a hot ice of tears, and she saw that small shadows moved in the room.

A chill rippled through her. She blinked back the tears and reached for Leroy, hugging him tight. He turned his head to peer at the room. Did he see these shadows too?

Shadows with faces. She drew a breath, held it, afraid to exhale: to complete a breath would give these images a reality, and to give them reality would terrify her.

At last she had to breathe out, and the shadows were still there. She felt the hitch in her breath. Dread pressed down on her shoulders. The shadows were getting darker, taking solid shape. Babes and children in strange rough clothing, their faces dark, most of their eyes dark, though there were two pairs of blue eyes staring at her. Spots stained the children's clothing, spots dark in the flickering of the tree lights.

"What do you want?" she whispered at last, holding a hand over Leroy's head to shield him from the sight.

"We only want to look," said one boy, the eldest, perhaps three. His eyes looked far older.

"Look at the ghostmaker," whispered someone else; she couldn't tell who had spoken.

"The ghostmaker?" Regina felt the tide of Leroy's breath as it pulsed past her hand.

"The next ghostmaker," whispered someone. "He will be great, and there is no greatness without its ghosts."

"Let us look."

"Let us wonder if lives will be worth his existence. If our lives were."

"Let us pray again for understanding."

Regina looked at all the dark stranger children, two-year-olds and younger, yet all with ancient eyes. She lowered her hand and turned Leroy around so that he faced the children.

A long still moment slipped past, punctuated only by the flashes of light celebrating a birth in this room full of dead shadows.

One of the shadows began to cry, then another. It was a wailing without hope, distilled despair of such purity Regina's throat closed. Tears flowed hot and heavy across her face, and there was nothing she could do to stop them.

Leroy's head turned as he stared at the sobbing shadows. The crying was so loud now Regina could not tell if he had joined it, though his body was not tensed the way it was when he was crying. She set him down on his back on his blanket. The phantoms shifted to make room for him even in the midst of their grief. Leroy's face was sad yet serene as he studied the shadows. Regina closed her eyes. The despair resonated in her for long moments, then slowed. The wails grew fewer, thinner, until at last there was just one voice in the wilderness of grief, and its sobs were slowing. The sadness lightened. When the crying ceased and she opened her eyes again, the shadows had faded. The tree twinkled as if nothing had happened. Leroy lay looking up at her with his beautiful eyes. She lowered her hand and he gripped it, his touch warm and comforting.

Ghostmaker, she thought.

*Herod the king in his raging*
*Charged he hath this day*
*His men of might in his own sight*
*All young children to slay.*

The terrifying impulse seized her to lower her hand on her baby's chest, to push the life out of him, force the expiration of his breath, so that the only ghost he would ever make would be his own. Save him from growing, save those around him from killing each other and saying it was because of him. "Oh, my son," she whispered, placing her hand on his chest, the crown jewel a bump under her fingers. "I love you." She pushed just a little, and he stared up at her, his eyes trusting.

She pulled her hand back, then covered her face with both hands, bereft of tears and almost of hope. She could not do it, not even to save herself from watching him collect his ghosts.

"Ga," said Leroy, and she lowered her hands. She touched his soft cheek. Mary means bitter, she thought, and finally she understood.

Ω

# WAGER OF DREAMS

## by Michael Rutherford

Once upon a time, the Kingdoms of the World lay enervated by common sense, conventional wisdom, and a growing belief in the value of things having value . . .

———— - ————

## TRUNDLE

Trundle had raised his tent with its spangle of stars, painted clouds, and fabulous beasts, hung the banner that proclaimed "Dreamer Within: Interpretations, Divinations, and Custom-Crafted Fantasies." But as Trundle had feared, business was bad. His only customer had been a pinched old man who wanted a dream of abandonment interpreted in a way that left his conscience clear to poison his wife. Trundle's crystal ball clouded in murky revulsion. The Dreamer was forced to usher the dotard out of the tent.

Trundle spent the rest of the day leaning against the staff of his banner. His attempts to look prophetic and oracular dissolved before the oblivious hordes that flocked from the neighboring kingdoms to revel at the Fair of the Summer Glut.

As night fell, the fumes of the sausage and spice-stew sellers and the smoky coil of the bonfires for the mass dances obscured the full moon. Stars blinked in the greasy dullness of the sky. The cries of the hucksters and flesh-merchants tangled with the wheedling voices of charm sellers.

Numbed by the variety of distraction, crowds flowed through the vast avenues of the fair like rivers of pale mud. Even the children, wandering in feverish packs, seemed enthralled by an enchantment of potent banality. Their faces were smeared with celebration foods, their arms clutched hoards of clothes, toys, and baubles. They roamed shallow-eyed and predatory — and, Trundle thought, as capable of dreams as caterpillars. But perhaps even caterpillars had their sleep seasoned with green-blooded visions of transmutation, of brilliant wings and flower-plundered sweetness.

Trundle finally shrugged off the despair that had settled on him like the myriad clouds of bloated flies. He stepped inside the tent, drew off his patched robes, gently slipped his throbbing crystal ball into a leather sack, and gnawed absently on a rind of goat cheese. His dinner completed, he tied the flaps of his tent shut, furled his banner, and walked past the terse array of the other members of the Guild of Seers, Speakers, Dreamers, Storytellers, and Non-Fanatical Prophets. Trundle exchanged grimaces and wan smiles with his fellows.

Dreamers had gone out of fashion. Few now valued the self-knowledge that a Dreamer could effect between the shadowed and sunlit elements of an individual soul. All that was not forgotten were stories and rumors of such malevolence, sacrilege, and perversion that even the people of these literal times shuddered to recall them. All knew tales like the infamous contents of the annals of the Dream Plunderers and the malignant catalogue of the tortures they inflicted on stolen visions. Even now, we recoil before the cunning evil of Charboos, who, as their mothers slept, drained away the dreams of the unborn and sold them to those too jaded or annuated to sustain their own.

The rest of the Guild had also fallen on hard times. Few at the Fair gave time to hear the ancient stories; even the Ribaldists sat silently on their bulbous stools, their inflated pig bladders limp in their hands. And the once popular prophets were ominously lacking trade.

As Trundle shouldered his way through the masses of revelers, he glossed their faces. Few there were that showed visionary scars or illuminations; few bore signs of the sympathetic magic wrought in the chartless realms of sleep. Imprinted on them all was a woesome urge for consumption, hungers of the most immediate kinds as they jostled and shoved in competition for satiety. Trundle wondered if this was a time growing barren, a world infertile or apathetic, so lusterless were the children. But there was little he or the Guild could do. The crystal ball bumped his shoulders. Trundle thought of his family and pushed on through the fair.

The light of the gravid moon blanched the spray of constellations. The road shone with the bloodless clarity of Trundle's thoughts. Abstracted by his plight, he did not notice how the air grew querulous, that coldness gradually usurped the texture of the summer night and the soft orchestra of nocturnal sounds bled to silence.

If, as was certain, his lack of success at the fair continued, he would become Lord Reedbock's scribe. His Guild training had made him skilled in reading and scrivening, and his teachers had discovered in him a talent for numbers that bordered on wizardry. His unusual practical skills had been bruited to Lord Reedbock, who periodically offered Trundle the honor of committing his noble words to vellum and of tallying the fertile prodigality of his domain.

If he and his family continued to starve on the wages of dreams, Trundle knew he must abandon the Guild and ply a quill on the ink-stained tables of Lord Reedbock's counting house.

With nostalgic self-pity, Trundle remembered his youth in the Somnolent Academy, the students snoring at their desks as they pursued their studies. How sweet it had been to slip softly into the dreams of others, tasting horrors, adventures, and romances in the ambiances of worlds relaxed from the gravity of waking life. Many chose never to awaken and were gently laid in the funeral barks pushed out into the Sea of Glass. But Trundle lived joyfully in both worlds, emerging from sleep with the vigor of a bee crawling from the calyx of a tiger lily.

And in the years of his training, he grew schooled in the interpretation of dreams, in the art of reconciling sleepers with the worlds that swirled in half-sensed sovereignty within all. So high was Trundle's integrity that he very rarely tinkered or trespassed. And it was not the fearful example of the dream thieves, whose corpses hung in the corners of the Academy with their nail-pierced skulls.

Quite simply, Trundle had grown to love his craft. And when he graduated, with high honors as Voyager, Voyeur, Savant, and Servant of Sleep, and his Masters shook him awake to give him his crystal ball, there was a quiet sense in the Somnolent Academy that here was one who would tend the dark gardens well.

But, Trundle admitted sadly, he and his wife now must change the instruction of their children. Rima, their daughter, already displayed an impressive, untutored ability in sleep-speaking. Taking after his father, her tiny brother Tock was a child adept of day-dreaming. These were not skills that would win them friends or favor in Lord Reedbock's hold.

As the shadow of a great leviathan will compound the darkness of sea depths and throw schools of lesser fish into darting fear; so a great, moon-wrought shadow massy with ill-portent passed heavily over Trundle, enveloped him, and finally drew on, blotting leagues of the forest, glided straight towards Trundle's ramshackle cottage.

The crystal ball surged in its leather sack on his back. With a finger-burning jerk, the thongs snapped and the ball fell to the ground and rolled before Trundle like a living opal. It furrowed the moon-bright dust of the road as he ran after it. In a lambent arc, the orb turned onto the path to Trundle's home and sped on.

He saw it burn down the narrow trail between the trunks of the great oaks, pause for a moment in the small clearing before the cottage. Then the front door hurtled open on its crude leather hinges, a jagged blossom of frigid light burst forth, the ball shot in, and the door crashed shut.

Trundle stood in the comfortless shelter of the trees. Green flames swayed through the muddy translucence of the greased paper windows. Glowing smoke clawed out of the chimney. Foxfire crept along the eaves, light that made the moon's shine seem sultry.

Trundle was not a brave man. But he knew that his family was clutched by evil. He followed the track of his crystal ball to the front door and stepped into the luminous ooze seeping onto the threshold. The door opened again. Trundle saw monstrous shapes backlit by corpsy walls of flames. The central figure held Trundle's crystal ball high in one clawed hand. The ball swirled with nebulae.

"Enter of your own free will, Dreamer," the figure cried. From within the house, the children screamed. Trundle sprang.

The cave stretched beyond sight. In the darkness past the fire's dominion, Trundle heard a continent of sighs, sensed invisible presences stirring in impatient audience. The open doorway of the cottage floated in the air behind Trundle. Moonlight laved the path beyond it, shadows of leaves trembled in night wind. The doorway was the frame of a picture of a distant world that hung in a palace of woe.

"I am sorry about pinching your young," the gargoyle said, "but we didn't have much time to get you inside. The magic is so fickle these last decades."

Rima and Tock sat at Trundle's right, playing dice with a skeleton. The pieces were its knuckles. Emilia sprawled in sleep on the cavern floor beside them.

"Your wife was most fierce in defense of the children," the gargoyle said in admiration, "she almost killed a few of the imps . . ."

A petulant squirrel-like chatter rose from the shades.

". . . so we employed a sleep charm to protect ourselves. It's love that conquers us. And rightly so." A great, scaly, bristle-haired arm dropped in comradely fashion around Trundle's shoulders. "There's a true way for all things, a proper tradition."

The mockery of applause came from flippers, paws, claws, scaled palms, and featherless wings.

Trundle beheld the denizens of all the thorned abysses that the Guild had ever plumbed.

As a farmer examines a fruit before plucking it, the gargoyle turned Trundle to face him. Trundle saw pleading in its eyes and a pitiless resolve. And Trundle knew he must barter for the lives of his family.

"We've come to ask you for help," the creature rumbled. "For in a way, your plight and that of your Guild parallels our own. We share the same tragedy: people have ceased believing in us."

The creature raised a great, taloned hand before the fire. Through the monster's flesh, Trundle saw the shifting outline of the flames.

"Every day, we grow less substantial as we lose our hold on sleep."

There was a dolorous exhalation of agreement from the hordes gathered in darkness.

"These last years, the dreams of men and women have grown stale, too narrow and brittle to sustain healthy fears and nightmares. Even children dream only of eating, of amusements, of objects they lack and how they will acquire them. The framework of dreams is being dismantled in an obsession for the waking world. Each soul slowly forsakes its dimensions and hardens. Soon even children will grow incapable of dreams. You and your Guild and we, the creatures of beauteous woe, will fade forever like breath stealing from the surface of a black mirror."

Lamentation echoed in the cavern, great teeth gnashed, fire rose in the eyes that glared around them. Trundle's children cowered against the skeleton's gleaming thighs. Emilia whimpered in troubled sleep. Menace congealed and cloaked them all.

"And what must I do for our mutual survival, most moral wight?" Trundle asked finally, when the din subsided.

His audience moaned approval. The gargoyle made an awful baring of teeth and grew more balefully solid.

"We will send you out into the world to return potency to dreams. For things have come to such a bitter turn that death itself seems less fearsome than dearth of possessions."

The skeleton with its naked fingers on the heads of Rima and Tock turned without speaking and nodded. In the depthless vacancy of its eyes, tiny stars winked. For a moment he lifted his hands and, where the bones of his fingertips had rested, the hair of the children was seen to have whitened. With an awful lurch, Trundle knew within whose arms his children found consolation.

Finally Trundle spoke: "For my family's sake, that of my Guild, and of course, my sympathy for your race, I accept this weird," he told the pair.

"Welcome, Dream Brother, a noble burden you shoulder and a great boon you receive," the gargoyle said. His golden eyes conferred respect on Trundle. "I, Tomec, give thanks for all."

The cold stone floor heaved, ground with harsh resonance in its depths, and then slowly became still.

"Others less generous, gentle, and fair than ourselves awaited your answer," said the creature. "They are satisfied."

Tomec clapped his hard hands; and, before the sparks from his talons touched the floor, Trundle fell into a fey procession of utterly alien visions and slept.

There were claws in his hair, probing his face. Trundle awoke and found one of the chickens on his head. He smelled the fug of animal dung in the packed earth of the floor, saw the smoke from the hearth hang as usual in the damp air inside the cabin. There was a homely reassurance in the muted dawn light resting on the lichen-splotched wattle wall. Behind him, he heard Emilia stirring the pottage, heard the scrape of the wooden ladle in the iron pot. Outside, Rima and Tock called in high, heedless voices to a playmate.

Trundle half closed his eyes and in the ritual way tried to erase the onerous memories of the nightmare that he had ridden during the night. Finally he relaxed and let the morning and the evidences of his senses lull and ease him. The cave faded, the gargoyle resolved to a pungent vapor that dissipated at his will, and his demon-ransomed family was restored. His sleep tamed, Trundle rolled onto his back, grunted his ease.

The great black bear that sat at their table rumbled in response. It turned slowly on the stool, stared at Trundle with golden eyes. The bear bent its head down to Trundle's face, caressed it with a sigh of brimstone that whistled between long teeth.

"There are certain changes in us that the sun has wrought," said Tomec's voice. "While you are about our mutual business, my friend and I will avail ourselves of your family's hospitality and offer them our protection."

Emilia threw a wooden bowl of gruel onto the table.

"Then the dream was true," Trundle half-whispered to himself. He walked unsteadily to the doorway to see if the children were safe.

"An answer unworthy of your Guild or your honor," the bear said reproachfully.

Rima and Tock threw crabapples at the emaciated old man sitting on the stump. Expressionlessly, he split them all with a glinting, curved knife as they whizzed about him.

"He usually has so little time with the

young," the bear said over Trundle's shoulder.

The apples withered as they fell and rustled at the ancient's feet. He looked up at Trundle and smiled. The banked, gapeless rows of teeth glistened and the sun cast his deep eyes into sockets. Trundle dully returned to sit across from the bear.

"You will return to the Fair," Tomec told him, "and initiate the restoration of dreams to the world. And from there begin your journey through the Kingdoms."

Knobby gouts of gruel hung from his muzzle as the bear spread a parchment on the table. The geography of the Kingdoms rose on its surface. Tiny rivers glistened, the spines of snowy mountains bristled, shadows of clouds slipped over the dark suede of forests.

"You are here," he said, pointing with a comb of claws.

A bead of blood sat in a black circle. Beside the circle, a filament of smoke rose, a reedy insect clamor, the hint of weasel musk and sweat. The Fair of the Summer Glut.

"On this map, we will be able to follow your travels and perhaps offer meager assistance if there is some threat to you."

Tomec placed Trundle's crystal ball on the table. It was black now, an orb of volcanic glass that threw a circle of twilight staining the morning. "There will be different dreams in these depths," Tomec said simply.

From beneath the table, he pulled a grey sack that writhed and darkly shimmered. Tiny squeaks and low chuckles issued from within. Trundle touched it in reluctant curiosity, felt the strange coolness, felt soft forms ooze and chitinous creatures scuttle. Pointed muzzles nuzzled at his fingertips.

"These are the last relics and seasonings of nightmares we possess," Tomec told Trundle with a queer reverence. "You will try to seed the dreams of the young," the bear said over Trundle's Kingdoms with them as you wander. If you fail, dreams themselves will desert the sleep of Men and all awareness and value will revert to what can be grasped while awake."

"What instructions do you have?" Trundle asked.

"We have faith in you," the demon said. "Follow your instincts."

Emilia called the children inside.

Trundle lifted Tock, then Rima to his face, kissed each. They ran out to return to play. Emilia embraced him.

"I will deal with these two visitors if you do not return," she whispered.

"I must start the journey if I am to end it," Trundle said wearily.

He slipped the black crystal ball into its pouch, lifted the slaty sack from the floor. It floated to his shoulder.

"There is little weight given to dreams these days," the bear said, looking up from the parchment. "We will be able to tell your progress from the map, how it darkens with the resurgence of visions."

Trundle bent over the table. There were splotches of shadow, mostly in the barren lands and the forests, where colors brooded like gems slowly revealed in a stream bed with the water's passage.

The demon answered Trundle's glance. "Yes, we still survive here," he said, pointing to the darker patches, "where landless and masterless peoples dwell: outcasts. Hunger harbors many dreams. But when life itself overlaps nightmare, dreams become tenuous."

But most of the map of the Kingdoms shone with a frail brilliance. The dark filaments of roads netted towns, castles, and the high-walled seats of power. Though, as far as Trundle knew, the map was totally accurate, most of the details flickered and then grew faint. The hues themselves floated pallidly above the surface.

"We are watching a world that dreams are deserting. You see the thinning of the very colors. So little magic remains that the map, a reflection of the King-doms themselves, gradually loses its definition. Only the darkness we both tend can return depth and value to it."

There was a faint gnawing and a tiny hole appeared in the map near Beulah Land. A pair of black antennae twitched and probed out of the opening; and then an ant with a chunk of dirt in its mandibles popped out, dropped the dirt, and ducked back.

Tomec growled with disgust, "Another city gone wholly bereft of dreams," he told Trundle.

Trundle saw that the map was pimpled with anthills.

The bear pressed the Dreamer's finger on the spot that was the fairground. Trundle winced in momentary pain and suddenly found himself inside his tent, the darkened crystal glimmering with malevolent sentience on the table before him, the dusk-stained sack writhing at his feet, and the noise of the crowd buffeting the walls. He staggered out into the daylight.

"Most impressive change, Master Trundle," said Bilial the ribaldist in the stall next door. "I never even heard the work during the night."

Trundle gawked at him, then followed the little man's admiring gaze and saw the transformation wrought on his own tent. The purple silk was almost black in the richness of its color. Phantasmagorical shapes and twisted faces rose to its surface, then sank back. Creatures crawled quickly across the glossy fabric, then vanished. At the corners, cerulean pennants snapped in a phantom wind that failed to stir the hot still air. And at the pavilion's peak, a lunar eagle slowly opened and closed its pale wings and sharpened its beak on the skull that crowned the silk. Trundle's own robes were cut of the same daunting cloth, and in wonder he watched a procession of grim creatures ceaselessly play across his ominous, opulent raiment.

"Gotten a new patron, eh, Trundle,"

the ribaldist leered with envy. "Quite impressive, though that fear angle's a little stale."

But before Trundle could even hazard explanation, the fifes, pipes, brazen trumpets, and kettle drums echoed down the Avenue of the Guild of Seers, Speakers, Dreamers to proclaim the insouciant arrival of the Parade of Triumph. On this last day of the Fair, a parade of nobles, wealthy merchants, sleek sponsors, prize animals, and contest winners snaked through every avenue of the fair, receiving the adulation and scraping deference of the less fortunate.

The winning Resplendent Vestmented Couple strode cheek to jowl with the Most Yoked Chicken, the Largest Ambulatory Boar, the Great Dugged Cow, the Feast Destroying Champion of the Table, the Young Vendor of Most Promise, the Elder of Most Inscrutable Promises, the Best-Groomed Children, the Master of Munificent Spells, and the Plumpest Family.

And at the head, as the host of the Chosen Gentry of the Fair of the Summer Glut passed in raucous satisfaction down through the flyblown avenue of the Guild, capered Lord Reedbock on his great white gelding. He squeezed a bladder of Karmelin wine and shot a purple stream into his wide mouth. Fat from the Feast of Triumph was shiny on his cheeks, and his flushed handsome face was at once a beacon and an icon of his companions' success. His horse suddenly shied as it stepped into the cool shadow of Trundle's high tent, and Lord Reedbock looked down with his red-veined eyes into the pale face of the Dreamer.

"A sudden change of fortune, I see, Master Trundle," the Lord said, surveying the sable panoply. The Parade of Triumph momentarily halted and bumped together behind Reedbock. The lunar eagle abruptly spread its wings, rasped its claws on the skull. The befuddled marchers were torn between admiration for the elegant equipage of the Dreamer and a certain apprehension at the bad taste of its mordant piquancy.

"I serve other masters now," Trundle replied.

"Well," said Reedbock with the oblivious arrogance of his position and a certain biting generosity, "a future built on dreams often dissolves into sorrow. I still hope to offer you the substantial honor of being my scribe when you fall again to earth."

Trundle bowed deeply and the shadow of the tent lengthened over the Lord, troubling his horse. A cold wind loped over the tent and billowed Reedbock's green velvet cape. He drew his mount back, waved to the revelers to continue to the laden tables of the final banquet. His mild annoyance at losing the Dreamer's services led him to cast a final haughty glance to slap Trundle into proper subservience.

But as Trundle lifted his face, a monstrous cataract of fear carried Reedbock away. The Dreamer's face was already dissolving in the acidulous effects of the Rotting Plague. Fatty grubs dropped heavily from Trundle's sleeves into the dust, the yellow foam bubbled on his lips and his lank hair drifted off his suppurating scalp: a pestilence so virulent that it was rumored the very glances of its afflicted were sufficiently diseased to spread it.

Lord Reedbock's spurs raked his horse's white flanks to blood, and they crashed wildly back through the packed procession of the gentry of the Fair of the Summer Glut and finally careened out the West gate and onto the road that led to his castle. The Plague terror sped almost as swiftly.

By nightfall, Trundle was alone in the abandoned avenues of the Fair. He silently assessed his smooth reflection in the shine of a polished shield. Reedbock's transparent vanity had provided the solution. When they had talked,

Trundle slipped into the shabby and sparse store of the Lord's heart and found his fear of disfiguring death, an ugly little creature that was the clawed memory of the last Plague that had eaten its way through the Kingdoms a generation ago. Trundle had drawn the Lord's imagination over himself.

Now the story of the Plague was spreading as fast as the fairgoers could travel. It would tremble through the Kingdoms like a fly's agony in a spider web. The last outbreak had been so swift, its symptoms so hideous, the fatality so massive that Trundle knew it would be weeks before any suspected or would trust to believe that there was no new Plague. The world was ripe for his quest.

But what was Trundle up against?

On the surface, it was a time of prosperity, if one did not count the outcasts. The roads were good, and the different products of the wide World sped through the lands, and the Weavers of Glacia tasted the succulent strawberries of Tusk, and the Horse Mongers of Stabul wore the silken garments of far Lathum. Choices widened, and unfamiliar objects and opulent customs waxed from novelty to expectation. The great Fairs, which had once been the seasonal celebrations of planting and harvest, expanded and changed into religious rites of barter. There was a bustle that wavered between energy and madness. Many of the Houses, Guilds, and Orders grew so powerful they were shadow governments within the Lands. Others, like the Guild of Seers, Speakers, Dreamers, Storytellers, and Non-Fanatical Prophets, whose commerce was in less tangible goods, slowly withered. While, as the histories say, most were not hungry and some few from humble beginnings could even attain auric renown, still there arises as we turn the pages of these documents, a stale and flagrant reek of satisfaction that seems the very atmosphere of these times.

Who knows if beauty itself fades without appreciation, for there are few songs from this epoch that the common memory has held worthy of survival. The writing, though copious, is a flat compilation of lists of goods, travel directions, and columns of figures: letters and numbers in servitude to the practical and the commonplace.

But there are other disquieting hints of the toll of these years. The charts of the heavens from this age display a monstrous simplicity so different from the generous anarchy of our own skies that we must assume that scores of stars abandoned light and the constellations reduced themselves. And we must believe their charts were accurate, for they agree through the range of lands, and this was a time when numbers and measures were used with a certain narrow skill.

In the bestiaries and catalogues of plants, we find with disbelief less than half the varieties that we now enjoy. They apparently knew few living things either delicate or fantastic. We learn the names of grains and fruits bred for market, but the range of flowers, their variety, color, and scents, is almost nonexistent. What kind of world does not have its air seasoned with the flights of dragons, its forests enriched with werewolves, its oceans mysteriously deepened with narwhales and mermaids?

But most telling is a cautionary tale found scrawled in the margin of a decaying treatise of the Sisterhood of Romantic Midwifery:

A young man and young woman of these dark years walk hand in hand out of the Bazaar of Love into one of the numerous private lanes laid out for lovers. The moon rises and they sit on a soft couch in a glade crafted for privacy.

He tells her of his family's wealth and his own secure future.

She enumerates her dowry.

Staring into each other's eyes, they whisper and fantasize the details of their wedding feast: their costumes, their invitations, the anticipated gifts, the courses of food, the desserts, and the measures of wine, ale, and mead, the properly impressive entertainments.

They live happily ever after.

## THE EAST

What ghosts there were in the abandoned Fair of the Summer Glut whispered with the voices of aggrieved merchants, hobbled like the jingle of coin through the maze of lanes as the wind shook suits of mail on their hooks in the Avenue of Armourers and rattled necklaces of pearl, abalone shell, and beaten silver in the Trove Shops of the Jewelers. Lustrous wool capes flapped on their pegs; susurrus rose from the ends of patterned bolts of silk. Partridges, pheasants, and capons crackled on still spits. Beeves blackened and dripped fat to sizzle in the throbbing glow of cooking pits. Wasps sipped from the pitchers of mead and ale, fell intoxicated to drown in their depths. Fruit flies swarmed above the goblets of wine. Scarlet canaries and love finches hopped nervously from perch to perch in their split bamboo cages. Kine lowed mournfully in their narrow stalls, speckled goats bleated. The great rows of trestle tables sat heaped with roasts, joints, chops, sweet breads, and split fowl, mounded with candied apples, clusters of grapes, quince, pomegranates. Bowls of gooseberries, currants, blackcaps, raspberries, figs, and strawberries rested untasted beside the glazed architecture of tiered cakes and the sweet bounty of chocolates. Beautiful gowns fluttered, diaphanous undergarments whispered unheard; boots supple with tallow and scented wax stood atop stands of shoe trees.

Night fell like troubled rain as Trundle stared into the depths of his crystal and poured his sight out through the points of the compass. Fire blossomed on the far side of the empty Fair grounds and grew with infernal energy. Finally Trundle slipped the orb into its pouch, shouldered the dark sack, looked back with regret as he left the tent, and made his way to the crossroads beyond the fairgrounds.

A cool wind soughed against his face, a harbinger of summer's demise, and drew the smoke of the burning Fair away. The night clarified. Great clouds drifted silently in the moonlight like castles of a celestial race. The sack writhed against him. Fed by the Plague terror, it was already heavier. Trundle realized that for a brief time, while the fear of contagation reigned, even those whose sleep was stony and reticent would be vulnerable to the dree fantasms he shepherded.

Trundle stood in the crossroads. The dark fields waited. In brief, bitter reverie, the smell of his wife's hair returned to him, his children's cries when they hid at the edge of the woods and dared him to find them. He assayed the luminous choices of the moon-bright roads and strode East.

The terror of the Rotting Plague permeated domains, townships, and principalities. Town gates were closed to strangers. Dogs and sullen men guarded the boundaries of great estates. Even the monasteries, usually islands of hospitality, had barricaded their entrances and nailed hex signs on the margins of their fields.

The caravans, companies of travelers, or solitary wayfarers that Trundle met drew away in fear, their faces averted, eyes hostile above the protective gauze that filtered the suspect air. The worst drew their swords, strung bows, or cast stones until he moved far off the road. Wherever he went, fear shimmered like the sun's weight on a beach.

But the East still harbored oreads, naiads and dryads, sprites and speaking beasts: living images which the earth dreamt and to which the indifference of towns and cities was anathema. Their existence meant these rural lands retained empathy. Trundle knew he must practice on receptive subjects until he gained skill and confidence.

That first night, Trundle stopped when he sensed the roiling of troubled sleep. He took the sack from his shoulders, hesitated in revulsion, then undid the hard, Stygian knots, drew the pursed mouth wide. There was a sigh from within, a skulk of greasy laughter, a burst of odor like the release of gases from a ripe corpse. Then a grisly flummox of creatures flowed slowly out of the sack, a saturnine blot, a gruesome fluidity. Transparent crabs, stinging winged atomies, crippled conversations, unctuous snots with nets of glowing eyes, things that humped like severed hands, mandrakes with the stiff walk of animated dolls, the filmy ghosts of mannerisms, decayed intentions, buzzing mites: all that were elementals of nightmare. Freed, they flapped, crept, scampered, or seeped away toward those who lay vulnerable in sleep.

What troubled Trundle most were the twisted faces turned to him in recognition, the mute thanks.

Trundle sat, while the stars moved in their pristine rounds, waited until the taste of darkness grew bitter. And then finally, he rose, remorseful and heartsickened to temper the magic of the wights he had released. This became the Dreamer's nocturnal routine.

Whether they had intended it or not, the demons who had enlisted Trundle had made a wondrous choice. There resided in him a rare integrity for the truth and temper of dreams. As he slipped from sleeper to sleeper, surveying the bitter potency of the spawn he had unleashed, Trundle tendered to each sleeper, from their own unappreciated, unused depths, the smallest tokens of hope or reassurance to check the black workings of the lamiae from his glistening wallet of nightmares.

Terror he left, and loss, and death; for these were polarities of life itself. But in children, he granted the faintest memory of awakening and light's return. And to lovers, when they were burned by visions of indifference, of desertion or injury, Trundle gave solace with love itself, its weedy resurgence, and consolation in the span of universes captive within the circle of an embrace.

And if most adults were less apt pupils, still when their children cried out in sleepy distress and they rose to soothe them: in that concern, there was a small breach in the self-infatuation that plagued most, and the chance of dreams worried the edges of their sleep when they returned to bed.

During the day, Trundle slept in barns or under bushes, the turmoil of the dark sack of darker visions his pillow. He stole food from sleepers' larders. Occasionally, when he was sunk in exhaustion, he found rich meals steaming on a malachite table when he awakened in a thicket, dew-drenched and cold. But if Trundle knew the promise of dreams, he also knew that he had been promised nothing. He was alone, as all are who honor their dreams. And the quest fed upon him.

At a table within a small cottage in a glade in a wild forest bordering the site of the Fair of the Summer Glut, a great bear and an emaciated ancient bent with satisfaction over a map of the Nine Kingdoms and saw the colors of the map deepen in the East behind the minute progress of a drop of blood the size of a garden spider's eye. And in the shed behind the cottage, where garden herbs hung to dry and wood for the hearth was stacked, Emilia the Dreamer's wife grimly sharpened a long knife on a stone moistened with salamander oil, while Tock and Rima waited with impatient anticipation in the small clearing before the cottage for the return of their two playmates.

With his shadow attenuated and drawn fantastic by the setting sun, Trundle returned a month later to the crossroads outside the ruin of the fairgrounds. The sack was swollen with new visions, the sleek legacy of his success. Dreams swarmed throughout the Eastern Lands. Centaurs had re-appeared on the Plains of Ennui. The volcano that rose suddenly in Datal had cast forth a phoenix. Pale rings of toadstools sprang up in the unseen glades of the Clotted Forest. Though fear of the Plague had dissipated, the capabilities of sleep thrived as they had not in decades.

Whether it was the strength of panic, the magic of his masters or the infertile venality of the Fair, the vast plain still stood blackened and bare. Only a dark purple pavilion stood where the Avenue of Seers, Speakers, Dreamers, and Non-Fanatical Prophets once had been. At its corners, cerulean pennants flapped in a phantom wind and a lunar eagle hunched on a skull at the crest of the tent, whetting its silver beak on the bone.

Late afternoon deepened to evening as Trundle slowly walked to the tent, the sack a malignant, shifting hump on his back. He drew the flap of dark silk open and dragged himself inside. The polished steel mirror on the center post showed him the face of a man who could have been his father. He sat down and, as had grown to be his habit, laid his head on the restless pillow of the sack. Though his family was in the forest that loured beyond the fairgrounds, for the safety of them all, Trundle did not want to return until he had fulfilled his pact with their warders.

He finally fell asleep and in bleak solace dreamt of Emilia, Rima, and Tock; of all their lives cleansed of woe.

When he awoke in the amethyst light of dawn seeping through the tent silk, he found on a malachite table not the usual rich breakfast and golden service, but a wooden bowl filled with Emilia's awful gruel, an oak spoon he had carved for himself years ago and small fistfuls of wild columbine, violet sorrel, and forest anemones, the stalks torn and mixed with grass blades; bouquets gathered with the indiscriminate eagerness of children.

When Trundle finished the meal, he took the withering flowers and threw them with defiance into the sack of dreams. He pulled the foul mouth shut and once more took the burden on his shoulders and stepped outside. A shaggy brown pony in the traces of a rude wagon of ebony grazed on the burnt stubble. The boards that formed the low rails of its bed spun with knots like the faces of gargoyles or of tormented galaxies spinning to dissolution in the void.

Trundle was beyond surprise. He threw the sack into the bed of the wagon, climbed onto the bench, took up the reins, and flicked them once. With a speed that belied its appearance, the pony drew the wagon through the crossroads and turned up the Northern Road. If Trundle noticed that the shadow of the pony loped with the gait and massive shape of a bear, he left the thought unspoken.

## THE NORTH

Like most Dreamers, Trundle had not forgotten or forsaken his youthful visions, but he discovered how much the texture of the nights had changed in three decades. Even as a boy, with latent, untrained skills, he had lain in his bed and the outrageous effusion of what waxed in sleeping souls washed over him like the wind-borne odors in the Bakers' Quarter.

But in the North, the darkness was untenanted, the winds merely the uneven heating of the earth, the small sounds only scurrying animals.

Trundle passed like a cloud. The ebony cart sped throughout the countryside without a driver, while Trundle slept huddled in its bed beneath the fabric of the tent, hard against the restless bulk of the sack of nightmares. So disquieting was the aspect of the spirit-driven wagon, its leering faces clustered and watching from within the umber grain of the wood, that none stopped or hailed it. With dusk, each night Trundle awakened to find himself outside the walls of a trading hold or a small castle.

In some few cities, when Trundle plumbed them with his blackened crystal, the sleep scent was like toadstool spores or a small animal decaying within a damp cellar. These were places of high commerce or great forge towns, sites where energy and avarice had slowly poisoned spirit. They were utterly devoid of dreams or their possibilities; and Trundle passed from them weakened, touched with doubt and dispirited.

But totally impervious sites were rare in the North. For the most part, Trundle found sleepers whose imaginations had shrunken to the waxy stillness of pupae. The children, with few exceptions, retained a stunted capacity. When Trundle released nightmares and misshapen wights to breathe fear, to whisper horrible lies, to inflate grotesqueries into full-fledged terror, he tempered them so there was always a scintillation of hope. Like invalids forced to movement, the sleepers gained quickened blood, agony, and the distant possibility of dance.

Perhaps it was the wild columbine, forest anemones, and violet sorrel that Trundle had thrown into the sack of abominations, or even the wisdom of the demons who commissioned him; but some of the dreams unleashed nightly now glided as well as crawled, caressed as well as rent. Ever afterward, the young created their own spontaneous visions and became saboteurs of the stolid frippery of this graceless world. And there was no price other than the slow attrition of Trundle's life in his concern.

During the day, the wagon passed through towns of muted wealth filled with well-appointed shops. Heavy banners proclaimed the seats of powerful guilds and the warehouses of trading combines. The faces of men and women were healthy, purposeful, and pitiless. Success directed and defined the land. In the bustle of the streets, the endless procession of wains loading, unloading, and hauling away, even Trundle's troubling cart slipped by unnoticed.

Beyond the last village, acres of houses crusted with rich ornamentation and shaped like jewelry caskets knobbed a featureless plain. Finally the houses thinned, the road grew less even, and — in a welcome aberration of landscape — a stream meandered in a small valley. The wagon pulled off the road with Trundle curled in its bed. The purl of water soothed his sleep.

Trundle had eluded the night patrols and stood in a lush commons in the midst of the banks of darkened homes. He knelt in the grass, crossed his legs, closed his eyes, and took measure of the sleepers. The moon sickled down pale light. Finally Trundle blinked, shivered, and rose. He could begin anywhere. Each house was equally desolate.

How right that in better times dreams thrived in bedrooms, Trundle remembered. But he found much less here. Beneath heavy comforters, the man and woman slept holding their pillows. Above each head hovered a calloused, leathery mass: a sum of embittered dream elements. Occasionally the pouches jostled.

This was Trundle's first encounter with ones stricken like these. He knew there were precedents for such monstrosity in the annals of the Dreamers. But he despaired of masterful solutions, felt almost fraudulent in this confrontation.

Down the hall, their daughter stirred in her room and Trundle inadvertently sensed her. He remembered the bony fingers on the heads of Tock and Rima. He emptied himself of all hope and approached the act.

Trundle moved to the window, where the moon lay against the glass like a scimitar. He raised his hand, pressed it against the pane. His fingers slipped through, grasped the moon's image, and pulled it into the room. Trundle stood for a moment, his face lit by the blade, then stepped to the bed. As if he were casting stones, he slashed at the swollen bladders over the sleepers' heads. A cloying foulness spilled from each sack and became a single aromatic scent as they mixed. In sympathetic magic, the deed rippled and was repeated in the rest of the darkened houses. The village shrieked. A changed silence resonated on the wind. The couple clawed each other.

Trundle flung the knife away. It flew and fixed itself in the glass of the window. The moon again minted the slate roofs to silver. There was comfort in the warmth of the blood that ran from Trundle's fingers where the frigid edge had bit. He left them in the pain and surprise of shared dreams and slipped into their daughter's room.

Her bedroom was an armory of toys. Rows of dolls peered down in frozen companionship from long shelves. The open closets were full of the splendor of velveted clothes, the froth of lacy blouses, doeskin shoes, ocelot jackets. The eight-year-old girl lay in the soft desert of her bed, around her heaps of stuffed bears, unicorns, griffins, and pigs. She stank of want. Her mouth was open in a half-realized cry. The restored moonlight haunted her black hair.

He read her sleep in mounting anger. It was like watching the hobbled grace of wild beasts captured for the pleasure of human eyes. Trundle brought a dream upon her.

She was walking in a forest, her parents riding on the path ahead of her, gradually distancing themselves. They dropped a trail of food for her to follow: dollops of lark-tongue pâté, golden apples, flowers of marchpane. It was a tasty game at first. But always, even when they were out of sight, their laughter and easy conversation floated back on the darkening air. She called lightly to them; their replies to her waned. They spoke of each other's beauty, the sheen of their garments, the satisfaction of their wishes.

She heard their voices blend into each other like a glittering snake biting its own tail. They still called to her occasionally in the flow of their words. But they were speaking mainly of her mother's horse, the new saddle she wanted, the probable growth of his trading house, where they were due to travel for pleasure, their daughter's tutor, the sustaining of sustained youth, their virtues reflected in their daughter.

Though her parents' horses ambled slowly, she was left behind in the narrow avenue in the dense forest of evergreens. Perhaps if she had brothers or sisters, they would have been with her and the loneliness diluted. They could have shared their parents' desertion. But the daughter knew, with a clarity that she would not acknowledge when awake, that her parents were never going to have another child. They were taken with themselves. Another child would change their own designs. And this was impossible. The girl knew she was the only child. She only felt needed because she had been expected of her parents. She was a valuable ornament of their success; a useful testimony to their kindness and humanity.

The abandoned girl trudged on. Her parents had run out of food to mark their trail. They were dropping articles of clothing, jewelry. The girl came upon a sapphire ring, two dark leather riding gloves, scarves, a lynx-furred muff, a single silk stocking. Her parents must have been many times naked but still the procession of garments stretched seamlessly into the growing shadows. Their voices had faded into the wilderness.

With night seeming to draw the sides of the road close, she heard animals moving in the woods, rustling the brush, and following her as she fruitlessly pursued her parents' relics. There was a grunt; she looked behind her. Her stuffed animals had grown huge. In a softly glowing train, they were creeping out of the woods and following her. The giant rabbit hopped beside the shambling button-eyed bear who drew in his wake the sea-gaited rocking horse and the scampering grey-mouse family. In the jostle of these animals was merged the host of the clothes and foodstuffs her parents had thrown away. Empty stockings hissed on beside eclairs, elegant boots marched in file with little oval tins of pralines. The procession voicelessly formed behind her and swelled until it clogged the road. She began to cry and ran helplessly in the night down the road after her parents. The animated mob lapped at her heels in mute companionship. There burned within her the realization that she was perhaps the only human being for leagues. In all these manikins of apparel, these gifts, these confections, she only desired the benison of another human being to speak to, another life with the eccentricity of breath, with eyes that irised for light or its absence.

And far, far down the road in the faint limning of the stars, a light flickered, went dark, and feebly reappeared. She ran, her past joys bumping behind her, ran until there were coals in her chest and her tears had traced the veins of leaves on her face. The fugitive light strengthened and finally she came upon a small fire crackling beside the road. The hunched figure with its face in shadow wore robes of glistening darkness, on whose surface ugly creatures scuttled and vanished. But her loneliness was greater than her fear.

"Can you help me?" she begged.

The figure lifted its face.

The nightmare pulsed and sucked on the child's forehead. Trundle hated the necessity of what he had inflicted. Its tentacles clamped tighter on her face and its tiny rubbery mouth covered her nostrils and drank her breath. It slowly sucked the poison out of her. The trembling girl's hair grew lank with sweat. Finally Trundle stroked the beast and it reluctantly gave up its embrace, fell to the floor with a moist splat, and sank away through the wood. Trundle gently placed his hand over her damp face and again entered her dream.

With a thin hand, the man drew the hood back. The girl gasped and for a moment forgot her anguish. The man had young eyes, but his hair was shot with grey. The play of the flames deepened the lines of his face. In his eyes was a surprised loneliness, that lifted as he saw her.

"Can you help me?" she asked him.

"Of course I can," the man told her. He smiled and relief grew in her.

"But it's really your dream, not mine. Make it what you will."

She believed him. Rather she knew he was right and she had forgotten how these things worked. Behind her, the stuffed animals snuffled, the clothes capered, and the food sent off overripe aromas.

She turned around without thinking and angrily said, "Stop it right now, you foolish THINGS!"

The garments, toys, and meals fell lifeless to the ground.

"That's quite good," the man said with approval.

Suddenly from the undergrowth behind him, a giant on a great white horse burst onto the road. The horse's hooves danced heavily and sent embers up into the night with the smoke. The firelight clung to the golden threads of his red velvet jacket. The giant's bloodshot eyes spied the small man hunched beside the fire.

"Give it up," he roared. "I have come to drag you back to the counting house." The giant wiped the greasy spittle from his lips with one rich red sleeve. "Rise, worm of dreams, little fraud of sleep," and he bent down from the saddle and swung a fat, bejeweled hand for Trundle's throat.

"Who do you think you are?" the girl piped in anger.

The gross figure paused and saw her for the first time. A look of mingled wrath and uneasiness quaked on his boggy face.

"Begone, child, before the business of men . . ." he blustered.

The girl smiled up at him with the smug, discourteous tenacity of a child who has seized upon a truth.

"You know," she told the giant with a cruel smile, "I don't think you're real either."

"Ohhh noooo . . ." Lord Reedbock moaned.

When the smoke cleared, a tiny white horse with a plump doll in red velvet rested against Trundle's dusty sandal. The doll's red bead eyes glinted. The two figurines were most cunningly conceived. The fire made the sole conversation for awhile.

"Thank you," Trundle told the girl finally. "Forgive me for letting one of my fears trespass."

"I hope it's gone for you now," she replied.

In the forest, she heard her parents

faintly calling her name. Their voices sounded frightened.

"They're lost, aren't they?" the girl asked.

"Yes."

"Well, I have to help them." She picked up a worn brown corduroy rabbit, a chocolate eclair, and a green wool cloak from the pile of her old things. "This is all I think I need. You're welcome to the rest of it," she said. "And thank you."

"Thank you," Trundle answered. There was a tinge of hysteria in her parents' pale voices now. "Just remember to be kind to them," he told her.

As she turned to go find them, she saw the loneliness edge back into his eyes. She hesitated. "You'll be all right?" she asked.

He smiled. "I'm better."

She knew her mother was crying. "I have to go," the girl said and ran into the woods. She had to. She knew the way out and her parents didn't.

Trundle reached into the mound of goods and pulled out a pork chop. He held it over the fire for a moment.

As he looked down on the girl sleeping at peace in her bed, he gnawed the pork chop in thought. When things happened like this, Trundle knew he was overextended. But with the resolution of Reedbock's apparition, he recognized, as he had not before, that he had committed his heart to the mission the demons had forced upon him. Such a multitude of thwarted children to reach, but the nights were long.

Even the generosity of the stream's trembling surface could not soften his reflection. Whiteness stabbed back through his long hair. Unlike the plague he had once conjured on himself to frighten Reedbock at the Fair of the Summer Glut, Trundle knew he could not call his youth back. Like a blacksmith years at the forge, Trundle had been scoured by the fires he used to soften and shape the obdurate elements.

He guarded as many of the young as he dared.

The geese in their migration flew barking over his head as they sought evening sanctuary in the marshes of the Kobak River. Trundle warmed himself at a small fire of dead apple branches. There was frost in the wild grass of the orchard, and the deer feeding on the windfall apples left dark steps. Soothed somehow by the fragrant smoke, he laid his face in his hands and rested. Then Trundle drew himself up, fell into the wagon's bed beside the great, tumultuous sack, and in darkness let himself be borne South before winter's arrival.

Throughout the Northern lands, in high canopy beds, on heaps of straw, children stirred as melancholy rippled through their sleep. And then they returned to their dreams.


## THE SOUTH

Though Trundle had spent over two months in the North, when the wagon dragged him in exhaustion to the Southern Lands, he found the harvests still being gathered in the final frail autumnal warmth. Each day as he gained strength he passed through great fields of potatoes, onions, and other produce, through vast ordered lanes of orchards where the fruit trees had been stunted so they could be easily picked. And everywhere he found families clad alike in dun-colored, earth-permeated homespun in ceaseless, weary gathering of the crops; man and woman, ancient and child under the direction of hard-faced men with cudgels, dogs, and whips.

Trundle would have attracted more attention, a lone man passing without apparent purpose; but the wagon moved swiftly, and the harvest was driven by the fear of winter's arrival and compassed all attention.

In a rocky, untillable copse, Trundle

slept in his purple tent for four days and gathered himself anew. And if any strayed upon the tent, the torrent of jagged-toothed succubi across its surface and the cold eyes of the lunar eagle on its perch of bone discouraged curiosity.

As Trundle replenished his energies from the attrition his concern and dream-tending wrought, he lay on the sack of visions. It had swollen to the size of a noble's canopy bed; the variety, number, and energies of its denizens multiplied by the resurgence of dreams. Riding its crest, Trundle could not recognize how visions followed him with the momentum of a lava flow. Within the sack, the dreams themselves had changed. While he had started out with an enfeebled warren of nettled wraiths, the sleep seeds he carried now were not all terrifying or tormenting. Whether it was Trundle's skill, the properties of the flowers that his children had picked and he had thrown into the sack, or the generosity of his demon sponsors, the sack now compassed the realms of sleep: madness and memory, love and death, hope and despair.

The Stygian hue of the sack itself had changed from darkness to the amethyst that lies on the cusp of dawn. The sack had grown from pillow to bed. And the voices in his sleeping ear now were not always the imprecations of imps, nor was what he rested upon the spines and knobby joints of djinn.

But as the sack grew, Trundle was drained and bent beneath it. If dreams once more washed across the world, Trundle was also bearing a wider world's dreams on his narrow shoulders. Even with rest, he was weakening, fading into the increasingly strong and multi-colored fabric of imagination. He was like an animal tamer who finds that within his cage, greater and stranger beasts are mysteriously being introduced.

Trundle dragged himself forth into the darkness. He slowly passed the long rows of flimsy tents and lean-tos where the families of gleaners slept in the barren despair of exhaustion. He moved on, the spirits of the sack twisting and mewing for hosts, on until he stood before the gates of the Fortress Farm of Prok the Flush.

And this night, as he never had before, when he opened the mouth of the bloated sack, Trundle winnowed the flow and gave it direction. To the families of gleaners in the featureless vacuum of their rest came the smells of certain foods, the tang of wind off a choppy ocean, a sense of place. In their dark sleep, dreams settled, sent out tentative filaments, and slowly stretched for light.

But into the hold of Prok the Flush, Trundle unleashed the original lamiae who had lain coiled and cold in the sack when Tomec and the Bone Father had first commissioned him: wraiths so malevolent that they had survived in tainted power in even a dreamless world. Trundle heard them ripple forth, saw the starlight fracture on gem-like scales before they dissolved through the walls.

Trundle stood motionless until the bitter effusion of the wraiths rolled out of the Fortress Farm in invisible waves. Then he walked to the great, wide gates that now stood ajar. No guards hailed him, no dogs barked as he slowly surveyed the courtyard. Even the rats in the depths of the storage rooms lay in stricken sleep. Nightmares had fastened on them all.

And when Trundle pushed open the bejeweled door to Prok the Flush's bed chamber, with grim satisfaction he found Prok broken to whimpers on the lisping sheets.

Before her confounding by the Zealots of Porphyry, Quezida, Queen of the Vampire Witches, had worn as the sole adornment of her cold, charnel beauty, a great snake, an emerald familiar that slithered and slid about her. So wondrous, fair, and prodigiously evil was this reptile that when Quezida at last was exposed to the rising sun and rotted to putrescence, the snake was stolen away by the remaining ghouls and nurtured until it was placed in Trundle's sack by the demons.

But now the worm of Quezida bound the porcine head of Prok the Flush, its blunt head nuzzled deep in his left ear. Like a diadem of crawling jade, the coils tightened and the edged scales slowly bit into Prok's forehead.

And when Trundle merged with Prok's dreams, he found gold melting away to doughy wax, nettles growing in his joints, a fire consuming the Fortress Farm, Prok become an ear of corn and the incessant hunger of rat's teeth feeding on his substance, vast holdings destroyed to calamity, strength and domination dribbling to pitiful ruin.

Without gesture or intercession, Trundle withdrew from the pillage of Prok's reason. He stood silent in the bed chamber and saw the snake sink its head inside Prok's skull. Trundle turned and walked woodenly out of the room, out of the Fortress Farm. He collapsed in the road beside his empty sack, enervated with the cruelty of justice.

Trundle dreamed of Emilia, Tock, and Rima bending over and over to harvest stones in a limitless dark field. They were three figures in a host of brown backs humped like loaves of bread. The wind cracked over them like the tongue of a whip. Split nails seeded the field with blood. The sun was impaled on the grey zenith of the sky.

In mid-morning, Trundle awoke numbly and found the sack swollen to monstrosity in the road beside him. The pony in its traces neighed as it grazed. The empty wagon stood behind it ready for journey. It was almost too heavy for him to manage, but Trundle finally shouldered the sack into the wooden bed of the wagon. He fell into the narrow space that remained and stared up into the leaden sky. They were winter clouds. The wagon lurched to motion.

In the frost-hardened fields, the gleaners wandered in confusion. The masters had not arrived. Some of the bolder set out for the Fortress Farm to demand food before they would work. Dreams of change stirred with troubling sweetness, with inarticulate hope in all of them, slow thoughts with deepening tendrils.

Back and forth, the gates of the Fortress Farm swung creaking, almost masking the sobs from within.

A pony with the shadow of a bear pulled a laden wagon down the roads to the West. Snow broke from the heavens like the breath of milk.

## MALCORDIA

O Malcordia of resplendence, Malcordia of fires, Malcordia of the spires. Evening catching your golden towers in a noose of night. Who has ever seen your like?

O Malcordia of the mines gouged into your breast; the ceaseless toil of the chained captives clawing out the ore beneath your foundations.

O Malcordia, where the dark, mephitic mills spewed out their comb of smoke and cleansed the air of the birds.

O Malcordia, where all that could be conceived was sold.

O Malcordia, of the minarets and the muezzin chanting out the litany of prices with morning's light.

O Malcordia of the great drawbridges, the fanged archways with their teeth bent inward like a python's.

O Malcordia of dark springs, hub of the wide roads, jewel of the desert, O metal-teated breast.

O Malcordia, storied mistress of merchants. Façade that launched a thousand schemes.

O Malcordia of the spike-crested walls, the merciless debtor armies, the iron-knuckled mercenaries sold into your service, the spoils-hungry warriors, and champions of leisure.

O Malcordia, of the vultures, high-shouldered and hungry; the thieves in your alleys, the cut-purses in your squares, the cries of the hawkers in your bazaars, the tiny hiss of the gas flames in the darkened stalls of the diamond mages.

O Malcordia of the broad ways funneled into your munificence like mountain streams into a gold sluice. So confident of your allure that all may enter the flashing gates.

O Malcordia of the dice, the gaming tables, of prodigious wagers and inspired chance.

O Malcordia of remorseless expulsion, of weed-choked pits where the beggars and broken were thrown each night.

O Malcordia, vortex of commerce, hive of trade, shrine of merchants, vampire of goods. Malcordia of passions and succulent luxuries.

O Malcordia of the sorcery of paper, of columns and figures. Malcordia of potentates on hidden thrones, of realms and races subdued with the scratch of a quill.

O Malcordia of gems slumbering in lightless rooms, of gold mounded in the dust of iron-doored treasuries.

O Malcordia of childless streets, of the slave markets spilling across the desert beyond the walls.

O Malcordia of waspish magnates crueler than pity.

O Malcordia, dreamless, coiled, and omnipotent.

Shall we ever see your like again?

Trundle lay in the wagon, his eyes resting on the first shy stars in the East. The wagon itself waited on the far side of the bridge that crossed the Scavian River, boundary of the domain of the West. On the far side of the river, the desert lay bruised with sunset. A cool, almost affectionate wind stirred Trundle's silver hair. The great **M** carved in the bridge's center pooled with darkness.

"It's done," he said to the pony, "decided long ago. Cross, gentle friend, and luck to us all."

The old man rapped the side of the wagon and the pony clattered to speed as if it understood his words. Even before they reached the sands on the far side of the bridge, scathing air broke over them. There was only one season in the West. Fever.

The powers of the West began to move. Though they were slow, they were not ignorant. Through the communication that their commerce engendered, they sensed a rising undefined threat.

And when the messenger from Queen Nonce was admitted through the gate, his signet ring read for its master; when he was brought before the one-eyed vizier of the assassins and the saddle bags of the white pack mules weighed, his message and mission were heard, and the confirmation was given of the acceptance of the contract, and its great initial installment paid. The vizier wound his way down through the exercise rooms where death and its delivery were daily practiced, down through the narrow storage hall where the poisons brooded in their cases, the vials, sacks of dust, and noxious herbs, down into the third level of cellars, where he pried a brick from the rotting wall and drew forth a tiny copper box crusted with verdigris. From the mouldering velvet he lifted the whistle of bone that his father's father had last touched, and with no small trepidation placed its noose of knotted snake skin over his own neck.

And that night, the vizier of assassins slipped out of Malcordia through one of the Guild's innumerable secret ways and, four hours before dawn, in the time of sleep's least hope and the night's deepest sway, stood in the sands of the endless desert, put the whistle to his dry lips, and blew one long, melancholy note pitched above the ears of men. As his lips cracked and the blood flowed onto the bone whistle, it sank into its substance without leaving a trace or stain; and the vizier of assassins knew the summons of the whistle had been heard.

When Trundle awoke, he found the fabric of the pavilion stretched above him in a canopy. Its hue had softened to the amaranth on the cusp of dawn. The creatures that played across its surface were less troubling to him now. He looked down and saw that, with his mission about to end, the sack of nightmares had shifted to the same gentler hue.

The pony continued its tireless pace. Trundle stood in the swaying bed and opened the flap at the rear of the wagon. The desert shimmered mockingly in all directions. A cry fell from the air like molten slag. Trundle looked up and saw the gyring of dark, stiff wings, gliding above them in the outline of an invisible crown.

He closed the flap, knelt on the sack, drew his hair from his face with freckled hands, and began to compose himself to face the colossal wrath that he felt gathering in the distance, like the prickly static and ominous hesitation one feels just before the heavens rend themselves.

Tock and Rima were asleep on their pallet. Two candle nubs sputtered on the rough table. Emilia fitfully scoured the black cooking pot with sand and watched their captors. At the table, the bear and the Bone Father stood silently over the map. Ever since Trundle had moved South, it had grown too heavy to remain hanging on the wall. Watery vagueness had resolved to the etching of palpable roads, towns and verdant lands. Minute winds feathered from its surface, bearing the smell of autumn. It was a world enriched to deeper definition.

The drop of blood that was Trundle had passed from the South and moved onto one of the great roads leading to the West. But apart from the fitful lines converging on Malcordia, here the map was featureless and bare. There was only the heaped dirt of the monstrous anthill that was Malcordia itself, the unfathomable scurrying of insects out of its dry mouth. And into the immense emptiness slowly rolled the drop of blood, like a poppy seed on a white marble table.

"Only the West and then he returns," Emilia said finally, venturing hope.

The bear's golden eyes flickered up from the map.

"Your husband was a greater hero than we ever hoped. Greater than we dared expect," the creature answered.

The gratitude in his harsh voice frightened her.

"It is better that the children sleep," the Bone Father hissed.

"You love him, and for that we owe you truth," Tomec the Demon continued. "We only hoped for a small corner of this wide world restored to dreams, a tiny sanctuary for us to haunt and survive in. That your husband could return so much of the world to the wakefulness of sleep was beyond our own dreams. We sent him to carve out a space for our kind and then be overwhelmed."

Emilia stared at the beast; bile, anger, and vengeance rising inside her. Her hand slid beneath her burlap blouse to the knife hanging in its leather sheath between her breasts.

"But now," the Bone Father rasped, turning his still face to her, "we owe him, life for life."

A sound like a cat clawing linen rose from the map. In the blank wastes above Malcordia, the fabric puckered, then split open. Green as poison, a tiny scorpion shouldered its way clear of the gash and onto the surface. It stood for a moment, pincing its jade claws, then scuttled lightly, crablike, toward Malcordia.

"All are heroes at a price, lady," the bear said in a flat voice, "and the greater the hero, the drearier the adversary. Hold your knife ready to judge us if we return. We leave now to try to save your children's father. There are many to call, many to gather."

And with great expanses to journey, the demon and the Bone Father sped from the cottage, past the blackened site of the Fair of the Summer Glut, and rushed with the secret celerity of all dark, foul things.

On the unobserved map, at the farthest compass points of East, North and South, fragments of greenness grew and slowly spread; and before the tender, inexorable strength of dreams, the sere clasp of winter slowly loosened.

To Malcordia, the fief of old King Log, where scribes and tabulators ceaselessly tallied the infinite details, destinations, and sums of the world of the Nine Kingdoms every hour of the day and night, the wielders of wealth, influence, and power came.

In the Chamber of Consumption, nestled in the twisted bowels of King Log's castle, utilized only in moments of utmost calamity, whose ebonite walls were sneak proof and word secure, whose gold door was guarded by giant mute eunuchs, Queen Nonce called the council to order for her husband, who wobbled in sleep at the table's head.

"Speaking for my husband," the Queen began, "as I always do . . ."

There was brief laughter from her listeners. That she eschewed dissemblance underlined the gravity of their convocation.

". . . we are faced with an as yet uncontrolled rebellion that threatens the commerce of our futures and the present foundations of our wealth."

All at the table nodded, muttered agreement.

"Each of you separately has indicated to me your concerns about a decline in the volume and quality of trade within your individual spheres."

"The rabble are not sacrificing to the deities of good fortune and gain," a temple archon spat. "If we are not religious, what will become of us?"

The banker Flux spoke for his fellows on either side, "Our customers grow less and less in our debt."

"And that, of course, means there are less purchases," Mothrah, czar of the trading houses, said. "The very roots of our existence are withering."

"The students don't attend to their sums," the scholar Bumble enumerated. "We have even found some writing poetry in the hours designated for study."

The list of infamies grew longer and more portentous as the other representatives spoke. Finally Queen Nonce raised a pale hand.

"I think I can summarize how far things have slid. In the last month, four children have been seen within the walls of Malcordia."

There was a shocked silence as the enormity of the sacrilege sunk in.

"Despite the codes of practicality, seriousness, and anti-distraction?"

"Yes," Queen Nonce continued, "the disease has spread even here."

The eunuch guards carried Prok the Flush in and rested the stretcher on the table like the exhibit of some herbal embalmer.

"You all know Prok, our boon companion from the granary fief of Roxilani," Queen Nonce told the assembly. "Even now we are struggling to subdue the gleaners of his kingdom."

Spittle dribbled from the corner of Prok's flaccid mouth. His fingernails burrowed into his palms. His brow was scarred with the cruel constriction of what seemed a band of chain mail. Shiny amber fluid oozed from his left ear.

Queen Nonce gestured and the mute guards bore Prok out of the chamber. Her shaken audience turned to her.

"Somehow Prok has been poisoned, his lands thrown into confusion and criminal rebellion. The menace we have piecemeal apprehended is now upon us all. I have taken it upon myself to call the Archassassin."

An inadvertent gasp of dismay and fear wavered over the table. Many cowered in their deep chairs.

"But the price, my Queen . . . ?" Garner asked the question that crawled in their thoughts.

"Would you have us loosen our grip on the soft throat of this world?" Nonce asked.

King Log roused, lifted his carroty head, smiled with vacuous amiability. "I think we will all join together in this time . . ." and drifted back to sleep.

His words dissolved in the silence.

"I know the price," Nonce said with velvet menace, "and I know what will happen to us all if the Kingdoms succumb to this contamination of visions and vile license. Let us vote now on hiring the Archassassin and woe to those who disagree." She lifted her pale hand.

With averted eyes, her listeners around the table slowly found their hands raised in concurrence.

"Call our Assassin in," Queen Nonce ordered.

None saw the Assassin enter. He simply was **there**. He was beautiful. He was young. His black hair fell to his shoulders. He was neither tall nor short. Even at rest, he shimmered with the possibility of motion. The deep red lips smiled on the pale face.

His five disciples stood silently behind him, the cowls of their grey robes drawn over their faces.

"The terms," he asked in a light voice,

"you know the terms?"

Even Queen Nonce seemed hesitant as she nodded.

"I guarantee success. For if I fail, I too will die," the slug-soft voice continued "I have stayed young for 39 generations. I have plied my craft once in each of these generations, been paid my price that each generation could afford only once, cheated age and decrepitude with that paying. And all these years, my craft and stealth have grown and deepened, the skills you now demand for your own survival . . ."

"I renounce my share of this compact," the scholar Bumble exclaimed in revulsion. "I have shamed . . ."

The Assassin's red eyes flickered to Queen Nonce. She nodded imperceptibly.

The dart caught Bumble in the throat, the stiletto his heart, the mist that issued from the Assassin's mouth peeled the skin from Bumble's surprised face. No one had seen the Assassin move.

"Please excuse this crude display as artistic excess," the Assassin whispered. "I usually work much more subtly with familiars, banes and noxious alchemies. But few who agree to my services renege."

The chamber was so quiet that the candlelight reflected on the rivets of the Assassin's leather garb seemed audible.

"My price," he rasped. "We have agreed?"

"As we agreed," Queen Nonce replied. Someone sobbed. "One life in four."

The five disciples sighed at once in hunger, in pleasure.

"Don't worry," the Assassin told the powers of Malcordia, "I prefer children."

And that night, when the Assassin slipped down into the galleries where his mages labored and raised eldritch cries, he smiled to find first payment made. His five servant zombies drew the treacherous, secret-pocketed garments from his young alabaster body. In a transport of eagerness, the Assassin stepped trembling into the mist-coiled onyx basin of blood. The mirrors on the walls caressed him, and he smiled at the perfection of his reflections.

The next day the Assassin watched from the walls of Malcordia as the mercenaries gathered and counted the slaves from the children's market and the captive pens that lay in broad encampment beyond the city. Children were forbidden in the city because of the disrupting empathy they fostered. When these unfortunates were tallied and then handed over to the magicians of the Assassin to be rendered, the lots would be passed among the citizens within the walls for the selection. One life in four was the price for the deliverance of Malcordia.

Finally the Assassin turned to speak to his five disciples. These were heroes from the generations he had survived, who had given their loyalty and might in return for endless life. In the execution of the Assassin's wishes lay the only hope of their existence. Past their families, their companions, and their ages they had survived. Now they only had themselves and the Assassin. Whatever joy that the Assassin could feel now shone on his smooth face.

"Once more we cheat the worm," the Assassin said. "Another generation pays that I may taste youth."

The figures bowed to him.

"Ready yourselves to go into the desert to scout out the arrival of this fell conqueror, this malefactor of terror."

The heroes who had outlived their own names and renown knelt in obedience. Their hands clutched the hilts of the great swords beneath their robes.

But then, with a cry of surprise, the Assassin turned and stared down the empty lanes of the Western road. With all the magic and secret wiles gleaned from knowledges of dead empires, faded religions, and forgotten alchemies, he cast his sight leagues out into the desert.

He stood motionless, slack-faced and confused. And then the Assassin laughed, laughed with the low, mirthless chuckle of a hyena.

It was the third day of the desert when Trundle saw his fate in the crystal ball. The images had grown clearer as they approached Malcordia and now he could read individual faces on the battlements. As Trundle looked at the lithe figure on the parapet with its five grey attendants, that figure turned, as if he felt the weight of observation and stared with his hot red eyes, stared from within the crystal out at Trundle. Trundle felt fingertips slip over his spent features, assay the silver of his hair. Then that unlined young face laughed with a fleer of its moist scarlet lips. The crystal squirmed in Trundle's hands, spidered with cracks, and shattered. Trundle brushed the splintered glass into the sand.

He lay in the wagon beneath the canopy of the tent's fabric, sipped tepid water from a goatskin bottle. The sack that filled the wagon bed softened beneath him. Wordless songs rose from it and led him to sleep. As he wearily listened to the ceaseless beat of the pony's hooves, Trundle knew that another day would find him before the walls of Malcordia. Like houris, like family members around a death bed, Trundle felt dreams about him, soothing him to rest.

Still laughing, the Assassin turned from the East and gestured to his five silent bondsmen to bring them close. Without thought he flaunted the cold perfection of his youth. The laughter left his face and he spoke in his remorseless beauty.

"I have seen our quarry," he told them. "He comes here at dawn to receive death from us. The rabbit seeks the

125

snare, the throat the knife. Rarely have we done so little to receive our onerous price. But such are the fears of our sponsors."

A silent cruel exultation emanated from the six, and the fell soldiers on the battlements shrank from the Assassin and his brood.

"Go now," the Assassin told them, "go and ready the execution of our payment. Tonight we slake ourselves and rise to sweet murder with the morning."

With gesture and command, with carnivorous wrath, the five sped away and organized with no hesitation, qualm, or question the gathering of the multitude that was the sum of one life in four of Malcordia, gathered them and delivered them to the mages and massed executioners who were necessary for the distillation of their substance into the elixir that would once more suspend mortality for the Assassin and his own.

The Assassin remained on the parapet, looking again out into the East. He had felt the breadth of what Trundle had wrought, its threat to Malcordia. But from history, memory, and professional experience, he knew that prophets and holy men were easy to kill. He shook his head at the ease of it all.

The crack of whips drew his attention away. Lines of chained figures flowed out of Malcordia and pooled around the slave compound. He saw the grey robes of his five servants as they directed the execution of payment. The Assassin stared a last time down the worn road that was bearing their victim to them.

"One old man," the Assassin whispered to himself. Then the hunger rose within him, swept away his mild amusement; and the Assassin glided to the dungeons where his magicks awaited his presence.

Morning broke over the desert like an exhalation of roses. In the deepest cellar of Malcordia, the mages chipped the six ruby chrysalides open, burned pungent

herbs under the sleepers' noses. Naked, in snowy radiance, the Assassin and his five liegemen stepped free of the crystallized essences of thousands of lives, stood graceful and grim in their reforged youth. The attendants drew over them the loose killing robes, crafted for swift movement, pocketed with poisons, weapons, and fatal instruments. With exultant swiftness, the Assassin sped out of the deep chambers, through the streets and to the great toothed main gates of Malcordia. Behind him, like great-thewed ravenous hounds at last released for the hunt, loped his five companions.

And out of the dawn, in a queer greenish haze that softly usurped the sanguinary light, came a small, dusty wagon with a canopy of amaranth silk drawn by a fat, shaggy pony. Down the Western road it came and drew up a quarter mile before the walls of Malcordia. A thin figure with long hair pale and fine as blown dandelion stepped from the back of the wagon. He dragged forth a great sack and stood alone with it on the hot hard cobbles.

Trumpets blared from the towers of Malcordia. The regiments of mercenaries yelled in derision from the battlements. The cry, "For the Nonce," rang again and again from the city and rolled into the desert. Finally the Queen raised her thin, alabaster arms for silence. Perhaps she and the councilors clustered around her alone apprehended the threat the solitary man posed. Her right hand fell, the portcullis was raised, the massive gate swung open. The Assassin and his assistants sprang forth and moved with ominous grace toward the man.

More than the mass of the walls, the jeers of the soldiers' faces, Trundle felt the huge, seamless preoccupation of Malcordia with itself, its monstrous satisfaction. In its smooth scorn, dreams found no purchase. At last it was over. He hesitated before opening the sack of visions, hesitated to sacrifice such beauty fruitlessly.

And the Assassin struck. With a gesture slowed to sight so its grace could be appreciated, he transfixed Trundle's heart with a poisoned dirk. As the slight figure folded slowly down upon the unopened sack, the Assassin turned to the walls; poised, posed in triumph. The cheers of "For the Nonce" echoed again and again into the desert. Echoed so loudly and long, that few noticed the tremors until the shouts had ceased in amazement.

For behind the Assassin, his arms still raised, his red eyes triumphant embers, a desiccated hand pushed itself above the sand. And another followed it. For a moment, they writhed like some awful barren shrub. Then they pushed downward, pushed until they lifted the rest of the skeleton out of the earth. With sand streaming from his hollow ribs, the Bone Father rose ten paces behind the Assassin. The pony who drew Trundle's cart reared and bellowed. Its pelt rippled, its body thickened and, in half a breath, Tomec the bear-demon stood with the Bone Father.

The Assassin wheeled as the walls fell silent, anxious to maim any who had diluted his renown. The five disciples swiftly arrayed themselves behind him. But the tension left him as he saw the two figures standing over the corpse.

"Begone," the Assassin said scornfully. He flicked the fingers of his right hand as if he brushed away ashes. "I am steeped in wizardry more wrathful than the misty leavings of one dead dreamer."

But at his words, the bear slashed Trundle's sack with one scything cuff, and out of the torn fabric there flew the thought-swift swarm of malevolence that Trundle had first been given. Numberless, ferocious, and with infinite agonies, they fastened on the five servants of the Assassin. The road, the desert, the very foundations of the walls of Malcordia trembled. The haze that had blurred the horizon thickened and slowly swelled to emerald cumuli.

Darts, throwing stars, and daggers bounced off the skeleton. Noxious vapors passed through him. Spells darkened the air and then boiled away. The Assassin emptied himself of wiles and at last stood in the novelty of terror.

With a voice like the scrape of a slab being pried from the top of a grave, the skeleton spoke, "Centuries have you escaped me, stolen lives from me, wrested false youth from others' blood."

He sank the bones of his right hand into the Assassin's chest, lifted him and shook him as a cruel boy will do with a frog impaled on the tines of a fishing spear. A torrent of blood gushed from him — the thick stream of generations sacrificed in a mockery of youth — spilled, and steamed into the moat of Malcordia. As the immense flow sped out of him, the Assassin jerked helplessly. Decay took root and despoiled him.

When the storm broke over Malcordia, the Bone Father flung the husk into the first cleansing buffet of rain.

O Malcordia, the songs are so numerous and vivid, so well-known, let us not recount the amazement of your fall.

We shall not tell of the miners swarming from the pits, their chains their weapons, of the Assassin's blood in the moat dissolving the mortar of the great blocks of the fortress, of the wolves who suddenly appeared in the streets and gnawed King Log and Queen Nonce, of the storm that coursed over the desert, restoring Spring in its wake, blasting down the minarets with its cloven lightning. No words of that fabulous host that shattered the armies of Malcordia, the horde of children scaling the walls, the harvesting the regiments of gleaners and ex-slaves made; the undines, centaurs, manticores, dwarves, and fauns who forced the gates. Let us not speak of the pillagers that bubbled endlessly from Trundle's sack, of the catapults of roses, of the furor of the grass as it grew out of the sands. Nor of the heaped gold and the unlit secret treasuries of gems wrought suddenly to clouds, to breezes, wild strawberries, and flocks of sparrows.

No, if you would hear it best, join the pilgrimage of the descendants of that visionary army as they wend their way from all the reaches of the Nine Kingdoms each year in late autumn. Go with them down the shattered Western Road to the high grassy barrow that was Malcordia. Revel and sing the ancient songs again; and in that place and company, when the last voices fade to sleep beneath the wide darkness and isolate, radiant stars, lie down with them in the long grass and dream.

## CODA

And so at the end, in darkness, the dark wagon sped back from the fallen city of Malcordia. Tirelessly in his bearguise, the demon Tomec pulled in the traces; and the Bone Father sat motionless on its bench, the reins in his fleshless hands. Trundle's body lay in the bed swathed in the empty sack of dreams. Finally they reached the ashen plain where the Fair of the Summer Glut had once been celebrated; and for the last time, its colors lightened, the figures slipping across its surface both nightmare and faery, the amaranth pavilion was raised to serve Trundle. Its head beneath its wing, like a nugget of silver, the lunar eagle perched motionless on the skull at the peak of the tent. The blue pennants drooped at its corners.

The two companions carried Trundle's body in, gently drew it from the sack and laid it on the cool floor. It rested there, brittle, aged, and pale as a husk of corn. With an awful groan, in an act he never repeated while there was life, the Bone Father reached into his mouth and wrenched out a blackened tooth. Tomec forced the corpse's stiff jaws open and with one fierce stab, the Bone Father embedded the incisor in the Dreamer's mouth. While they watched through the long night and a wind swollen with phantasmagoria brushed

the tent, a measure of life and youth returned to Trundle.

It was almost Trundle who walked through the cottage door at dawn the next morning. Enough that Emilia cried out and wept, and that Tock and Rima ran to him in their transport of sudden joy. But when Emilia relinquished her embrace and let the children swarm upon the dazed figure, she looked hard at him for the first time and knew that it was not simply that he had grown frail.

While the children besieged their father, on the floor Emilia saw the shadows of two figures who stood beyond the door. She walked out and found Tomec and the Bone Father waiting.

"We restored what we were able," Tomec told her.

The Bone Father spat blood against an oak trunk. "A gift I will never again bestow," he groaned.

Rot bored through the tree. Yellow leaves fell around them.

"Go," she said to them, "while my anger and gratitude are confused."

"For your hospitality," the bear replied, bowing, irony in his golden eyes.

The two figures walked from the cottage into the shadow of the forest. The path opened like a wound before them, and before they descended into the comfort of the flames, their sun-ordained shapes fell from them. For one crawling instant, Emilia saw the true lineaments of Death and the Prince of Nightmares. Then the morning light brought warmth to her again, and she returned to the cottage.

If sometimes the sun seemed to shine through Trundle, still his children knew that most parents were transparent and lacked definition a good portion of the time.

And after those nights when Trundle was so abstracted that he was no more than a breath upon her face in the dark, the weight of thistledown in her arms,

Emilia would walk at dawn among the oak trees to where she had laid the map that had been the record of his journey through the Kingdoms. In that radiant cartography, she read anew the price Trundle had paid, voluntarily and of necessity, and realized the generous spectrum of his shade.  Ω

# Weirdisms

**HELL and DAMNATION** inevitably await the sorcerer, no matter how powerful he is or how great the promises made to him. The infernal bargain he made will damn him eternally.